W9-CBU-719

# EYEWITNESS BOOKS

# DOG

Great Dane puppies

Bloodhound

Red fox

Skeleton of
maned wolf

Australian silky terrier

Shampooed
poodle

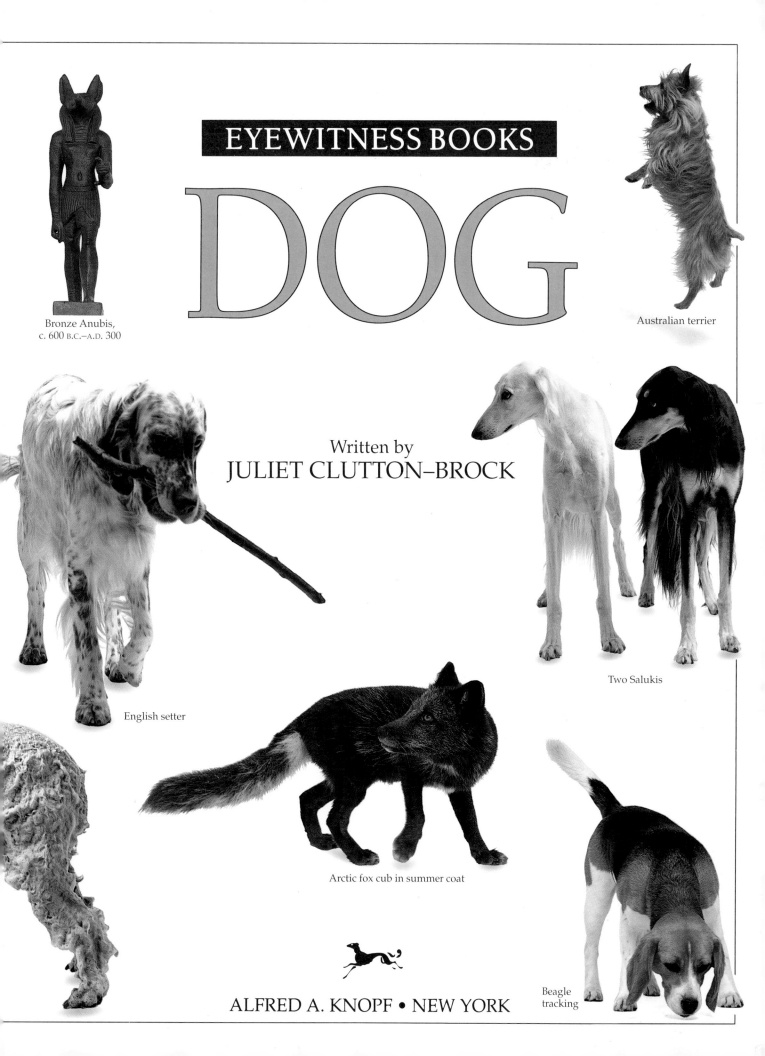

# EYEWITNESS BOOKS

# DOG

Written by
JULIET CLUTTON–BROCK

Bronze Anubis,
c. 600 B.C.–A.D. 300

Australian terrier

Two Salukis

English setter

Arctic fox cub in summer coat

Beagle
tracking

ALFRED A. KNOPF • NEW YORK

Long-haired and miniature wire-haired dachshunds

Arctic fox in winter coat

Skull of fennec fox

Crossbred dog

Lurcher

**Project editor** Marion Dent
**Art editor** Jutta Kaiser-Atcherley
**Senior editor** Helen Parker
**Senior art editor** Julia Harris
**Production** Louise Barratt
**Picture research** Cynthia Hole
**Special photography** Jerry Young, Alan Hills of the British Museum, Colin Keates of the Natural History Museum

This is a Borzoi Book published by Alfred A. Knopf, Inc.

This Eyewitness Book has been conceived by Dorling Kindersley Limited and Editions Gallimard

First American edition, 1991

Copyright © 1991 Dorling Kindersley Limited, London. All rights reserved under International and Pan-American Copyright Conventions. Published in the United States by Alfred A. Knopf, Inc., New York. Distributed by Random House, Inc., New York. Published in Great Britain by Dorling Kindersley Limited, London.

Manufactured in Singapore  0 9 8 7 6 5 4 3 2 1

**Library of Congress Cataloging-in-Publication Data**
Clutton-Brock, Juliet.
Dog / written by Juliet Clutton-Brock.
p. cm.– (Eyewitness books)
Includes index.
Summary: Text and photographs highlight the evolutionary history of dogs, their domestication, anatomy, behavior, and breeds. Offers guidance on dog care and training.
1. Dogs – Juvenile literature.
2. Dog breeds – Juvenile literature.
3. Working dogs – Juvenile literature.
[1. Dogs.  2. Dog breeds.  3. Working dogs.]
I. Title.
SF426.5.C58  1991
599.74'442–dc20  91-10135
ISBN 0-679-81459-0
ISBN 0-679-91459-5 (lib. bdg.)

Color reproduction by Colourscan, Singapore
Printed in Singapore by Toppan

Bronze dog from Egypt, c. 300 B.C.–A.D. 300

French bulldog

Roman bronze lamp (composite of dog's head and feet), 1st century B.C.– 1st century A.D.

# Contents

Boxer

# What is a dog?

**PRAYING FOR PREY**
St. Hubert, patron saint of hunters, is shown with his hounds by German painter Albrecht Dürer (1471–1528).

T HE DOG FAMILY, called Canidae from the Latin *canis* meaning "dog," includes approximately 37 species of wolves, jackals, foxes, and wild and domestic dogs. All members of the dog family, or canids, are carnivores (meat eaters) and have special adaptations for hunting. Their teeth (pp. 8–9) are used for killing prey, chewing meat, and gnawing bones – and sometimes for fighting each other. Their highly developed senses of sight, sound, and smell (pp. 14–17) –  with their large eyes, erect ears, and sensitive noses – mean they can track prey successfully, whether they are social or solitary hunters (pp. 18–19). All wild dogs, except for the South American bush dog (pp. 32–33), have long legs adapted for running fast in pursuit of prey. All canids are "digitigrade" (they walk on their toes) and have distinctive feet, with five claws on the front foot and four on the hind. In domestic dogs, there is sometimes an extra, fifth claw (dewclaw) on the hind foot. Wild dogs have long tails, and their dense fur is usually a solid color without spots or stripes (pp. 12–13). Canids mate once a year, and after two months' development in the womb, a litter of pups is born (pp. 20–21). Like all mammals, the mother suckles her young after they are born and cares for them for several months, with help from the rest of the family.

**DISTRIBUTION OF DOGS**
Wild canids originally lived in every continent of the world, except Australasia, where they have been introduced by humans (pp. 36–37), and Antarctica.

North America

Europe

Asia

Africa

South America

Australia

*Coat is multicolored and distinctive*

*Ears are small, erect, and rounded*

**THE JOVIAL JACKAL**
There are four species of jackal (pp. 24–25) – the golden, the side-striped, the black-backed, and the Simien. All of the species live in Africa, but the golden also lives in parts of Europe and Asia. Jackals live and hunt in pairs and usually stay together for life.

Golden jackal

*Bushy tail, or brush*

**RED SOLITAIRE**
The red fox is a solitary hunter of rabbits and rodents. The fox is the only canid that does not hunt in a pack (pp. 28–29). The most characteristic part of the fox is its bushy tail.

Red fox

## DOGGIES OF ALL SORTS

Dogs have been bred in an amazing assortment of shapes, sizes, and colors. This painting shows just some of the 400 breeds of domestic dogs (pp. 48–61) in the world. All these breeds are descended from the wolf, which was first tamed by humans about 12,000 years ago (pp. 8–9).

## WARM FEET

Of the many ways dogs have helped people, one of the more unusual ones was as a foot warmer for church congregations in the Middle Ages. Shown in this beautiful stained glass (right) are the biblical characters Tobias and Sarah – and their dog.

*Teeth number the usual 42 (pp. 8–9), but first lower molars are small and flat – unlike other dogs' teeth*

## THE LARGEST CANID

The wolf (pp. 22–23) is the largest of all the wild canids. It lives and hunts in a family group, or pack, and is the most social (pp. 18–19) of all the carnivores. The wolf is the ancestor of all domestic dogs (pp. 48–61).

This wolf has thick gray fur, but the fur can vary from nearly pure white to red to brown or black

Gray wolf

## AFRICAN HUNTER

The African hunting dog is a highly developed social carnivore (pp. 18–19) that hunts in family groups. These wild dogs live in the grasslands of Africa (pp. 26–27), but are in danger of extinction. Great numbers of them are being hunted and poisoned by farmers; they are also dying from disease, particularly canine distemper.

African hunting dog

*Shorter hind legs give typical crouching position*

*Muzzle was heavy, and its teeth were very different from a dog's*

This striped hyena is found in Africa and western Asia. Hyenas are hunters and scavengers; their powerful teeth can crush bones that even big cats are not able to chew.

*Long, powerful front legs*

The Tasmanian wolf looked similar to a dog, but it was a marsupial and unrelated to the dog family. It is now known only from stuffed specimens in museums.

*Rounded ears*

*Thick, muscular base of tail could not wag like a dog's*

# What is not a dog?

Sometimes called dogs, the hyena, Tasmanian wolf, and prairie dog are not in the dog family. The three species of hyena, within the Hyaenidae family, are more closely related to cats. The Tasmanian wolf, or thylacine, now extinct, was a marsupial (pouched mammal) that lived in Australia, and the North American prairie dog is a rodent related to squirrels.

Prairie dogs are highly social rodents that live in communal burrows covering up to 160 acres.

# Evolution of the dog family

THIRTY MILLION YEARS AGO, during the Oligocene period, the first doglike creature, *Cynodictis* (a mongoose-like animal with a long muzzle), appeared on Earth. It replaced the earlier widespread group of carnivores – the creodonts. All the earliest fossils of the dog family have been found in North America and date from this period. Another canid-like carnivore, *Tomarctus*, evolved during the Miocene period, about 24 million years ago. In turn, the genus *Canis* evolved, which gradually developed into *Canis lupus*, or the wolf, some 300,000 years ago. The first domestic dogs date from around 12,000 years ago. There were also creatures that looked similar to these dog ancestors, such as the hyaenodonts from the Oligocene, but they were not related to true hyenas, which are closer to the cat family. From ancestral carnivores like *Cynodictis*, the canids evolved into fast-running meat eaters that hunted prey on open grasslands, and most of today's living species have inherited this way of life.

**BE SIRIUS**
The brightest star in the sky is the Dog Star (Sirius) in the Canis Major constellation. Just as vast changes have taken place over millions of years in space, so the family of dogs has evolved over millions of years on Earth.

*Cranium (brain box)*

*Nasal bone*

*Upper jaw bone*

*Orbit for eye*

*Ear bone*

*Upper carnassial tooth for tearing flesh*

*Foramen magnum – entrance for the spinal cord to the brain*

Side view of *Cynodictis* skull

*Cranium*

*Orbit*

*Upper molar*

*Palatal bone*

Palatal view of *Cynodictis* skull

**THIRTY-MILLION-YEAR-OLD HEAD**
This is the fossilized skull of one of the ancestors of the dog family. It was a mongoose-like animal called *Cynodictis*, and it lived about 30 million years ago.

**DIRE CONSEQUENCES**
The extinct dire wolf (below) lived in California during the period of the Ice Ages. It was huge – much larger than any living wolf – and it preyed on the mammoth and other large Ice Age mammals.

Restoration of dire wolf

Reconstruction of a scene at the tar pits of La Brea near Los Angeles, showing dire wolves and a *Smilodon* attacking a mammoth (right)

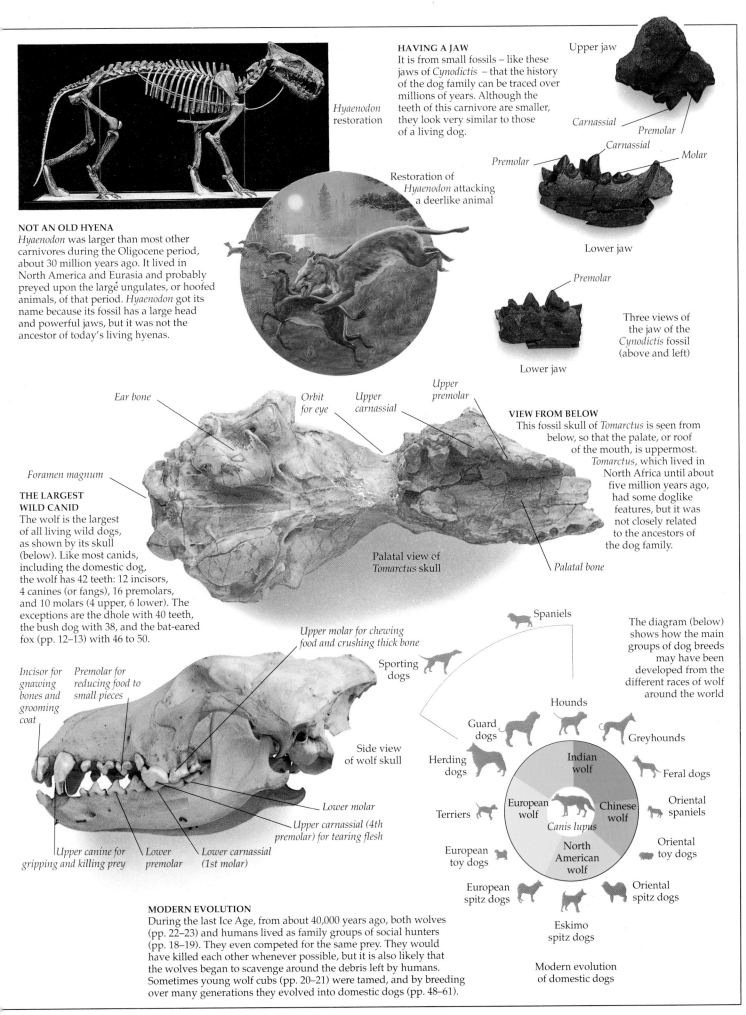

**HAVING A JAW**
It is from small fossils – like these jaws of *Cynodictis* – that the history of the dog family can be traced over millions of years. Although the teeth of this carnivore are smaller, they look very similar to those of a living dog.

*Hyaenodon* restoration

Upper jaw

*Carnassial*
*Premolar*

*Premolar*
*Carnassial*
*Molar*

Lower jaw

Restoration of *Hyaenodon* attacking a deerlike animal

*Premolar*

Three views of the jaw of the *Cynodictis* fossil (above and left)

Lower jaw

**NOT AN OLD HYENA**
*Hyaenodon* was larger than most other carnivores during the Oligocene period, about 30 million years ago. It lived in North America and Eurasia and probably preyed upon the large ungulates, or hoofed animals, of that period. *Hyaenodon* got its name because its fossil has a large head and powerful jaws, but it was not the ancestor of today's living hyenas.

Ear bone
*Orbit for eye*
*Upper carnassial*
*Upper premolar*

Foramen magnum

**VIEW FROM BELOW**
This fossil skull of *Tomarctus* is seen from below, so that the palate, or roof of the mouth, is uppermost. *Tomarctus*, which lived in North Africa until about five million years ago, had some doglike features, but it was not closely related to the ancestors of the dog family.

**THE LARGEST WILD CANID**
The wolf is the largest of all living wild dogs, as shown by its skull (below). Like most canids, including the domestic dog, the wolf has 42 teeth: 12 incisors, 4 canines (or fangs), 16 premolars, and 10 molars (4 upper, 6 lower). The exceptions are the dhole with 40 teeth, the bush dog with 38, and the bat-eared fox (pp. 12–13) with 46 to 50.

Palatal view of *Tomarctus* skull

*Palatal bone*

Spaniels

The diagram (below) shows how the main groups of dog breeds may have been developed from the different races of wolf around the world

*Upper molar for chewing food and crushing thick bone*

Sporting dogs

Hounds

Guard dogs

Greyhounds

*Incisor for gnawing bones and grooming coat*
*Premolar for reducing food to small pieces*

Herding dogs

Indian wolf

Feral dogs

Side view of wolf skull

Terriers

European wolf

Chinese wolf

Oriental spaniels

*Canis lupus*

European toy dogs

North American wolf

Oriental toy dogs

*Lower molar*

*Upper carnassial (4th premolar) for tearing flesh*

European spitz dogs

Oriental spitz dogs

*Upper canine for gripping and killing prey*
*Lower premolar*
*Lower carnassial (1st molar)*

Eskimo spitz dogs

Modern evolution of domestic dogs

**MODERN EVOLUTION**
During the last Ice Age, from about 40,000 years ago, both wolves (pp. 22–23) and humans lived as family groups of social hunters (pp. 18–19). They even competed for the same prey. They would have killed each other whenever possible, but it is also likely that the wolves began to scavenge around the debris left by humans. Sometimes young wolf cubs (pp. 20–21) were tamed, and by breeding over many generations they evolved into domestic dogs (pp. 48–61).

# Dogs' bones

**OLD MOTHER HUBBARD**
This familiar nursery rhyme crone
has no bones for her dog to chew
(pp. 62–63) – "her cupboard is bare."

T HE SKELETON OF A MAMMAL provides the
solid framework on which the rest of the
body is built. The bones of the skull protect
the brain, mouth, eyes, nose, and ears. The
backbone supports the heart, lungs, and
digestive system. The shoulder blade
and hip girdle are the pivots that
allow the limb bones to move.
Attached to the ends of the bones
are ligaments and tendons, which
act like strong elastic to keep them joined together yet
movable. Muscles are also attached to the bones in a
complicated system that enables the body to move in
all directions. Each bone in a canid's skeleton has
characteristics that make it recognizable as
belonging to a member of the dog family.
Wolves, dogs (both wild and domestic),
and foxes have long skulls and large
teeth. The neck and the backbone are
also relatively long, the ribs form a
strong cage to protect the chest,
and the long limb bones are
adapted for fast running.

*Skull of a
wolf can always be
recognized by the large size of
the tearing, or carnassial, teeth*

**LARGE AS LIFE**
Apart from some giant domestic
dogs, the wolf (pp. 22–23)
has the largest
skeleton of all
the animals
in the dog
family.

Arctic
wolf

*Neck
vertebrae*

*Sternum*

**AFRICAN HUNTER**
The African hunting dog
(pp. 26–27) has very long legs in
relation to the size of its body, so
it is able to range over huge
distances in search of prey.

African hunting dog

*Elbow
joint*

*Radius*

*Ulna*

Red
fox

**LITTLE RED**
The red fox spends much of its
time creeping under bushes and
rocks. It has shorter legs in
relation to the size of its body
than the wolf does.

*Pelvis*

*Tibia*

*Radius*

*Elbow joint*

*Ulna*

Skeleton of red fox

*Hock, or
ankle joint*

Skeleton of African hunting dog

*Round skull*

*Lower
jaw*

*Shoulder
joint*

*Sternum*

*Metacarpal
bone*

Skeleton of
Maltese dog

**BALL OF FLUFF**
This fluffy Maltese dog
does not look at all like a
wolf, but inside its skin
the skeleton is just like
that of a tiny wolf.

*Neck is short,
but still has
seven vertebrae*

Maltese dog

*Vertebrae in the neck have very powerful muscle attachments, enabling the wolf to bring down and kill its prey*

*Scapula, or shoulder blade*

*Pelvis, or hip*

**ONE LEFT FOOT**
So that the wolf can walk on its toes, the bones of the feet are extended.

*Digit, or first toe, is shorter and not used for walking*

*Carpal bone, or wrist bone*

*Last pairs of ribs are said to be "floating" because they are not attached to the sternum, or breastbone*

*Metacarpal bone, or toe bone*

*Tail bone*

*High knee gives the greatest length to leg and foot*

*Claw*

Left front foot of North American wolf

*Sternum, or breastbone, is made of soft bones and cartilage, so it can move as the wolf breathes*

*Hock, or ankle joint, has very strong attachments for the ligaments*

*Hind foot has only four toes – there is no dewclaw (pp. 6–7) in wild canids*

**KEEPING TRACKS**
These large-sized tracks show that a wolf has recently crossed the snow-packed Arctic tundra in northern Canada.

Skeleton of North American wolf

*Femur*

German shepherd

*Orbital muscle*

*Neck muscle*

*Shoulder muscle*

*Tongue*

*Backbone*

*Kidney*

*Jaw muscles*

**PUMPING IRON**
The muscles encase the skeleton and give it flexibility. They are fueled by oxygen in the blood.

*Throat muscle*

*Bladder*

*Trachea*

**THE INSIDE STORY**
The lungs breathe in oxygen, which is picked up by the blood and pumped around the body by the heart. The stomach receives food, which supplies energy to the dog, and waste products are excreted through the large intestine.

*Chest muscle*

*Small intestine*

*Heart*

*Ligaments of foot*

*Arm muscle*

*Tail bone*

*Stomach*

*Duodenum*

Internal organs of German shepherd

Muscle system of German shepherd

# Coats, heads, and tails

A DOG'S FUR IS NECESSARY to keep the dog warm; its fur is denser in cold climates, and shorter in hot ones. It is composed of two layers: an undercoat of fine wool, usually of one color, and a top coat of longer, coarser hairs, called guard hairs, which have natural oils that make the coat waterproof. The top coat carries the brindled, or striped, pattern of the fur. The heads of all wild dogs look very much alike. Whether large like the wolf or small like the bat-eared fox, all wild canids have long heads with erect ears, and teeth set in a line along straight jaws. Tails too are all similar – long, straight, often bushy, with a white or black tip. The tail is one of a dog's most important assets and is used for balancing when running fast, for expressing the dog's feelings, and for signaling to other members of the pack. When dogs were domesticated, their appearance changed because certain features were specially selected for each breed. For example, no wild dog has a tail permanently curled over its back.

**FUR COATS**
Before the present century, for people to keep warm in the winter it was essential to have clothing made from animal furs. Today, with all the artificial materials available, wearing a fur coat shows that the person has no regard for the dwindling numbers of wild animals and little compassion for their suffering.

Tails of many domestic dogs – like this Australian terrier (pp. 52–53) – are docked so that the tail stands up straight

Tail of the red fox (pp. 28–29) is always reddish and bushy and is referred to as a brush

Thick tail of Bernese mountain dog (pp. 56–57) keeps it warm

Gray tree fox (pp. 28–29) has typically soft gray fur (left)

Sand fox (pp. 30-31) lives in very hot places and has fine, dense fur (above)

African hunting dog (pp. 26–27) has short hair (above) so it does not get too hot when running

Dachshunds (pp. 48–49) can be long-haired (right), short-haired, or wire-haired (far right)

Wirehair of a miniature dachshund (above)

Dalmatian's (pp. 54–55) tail even has spots on it

Hairy tail of giant schnauzer is cut short by docking (pp. 44–45)

**LOSING THEIR HAIR**
Most wild and domestic dogs shed every spring and autumn, so they have a thin coat in the summer and a thick one in the winter. The fur of this German shepherd (pp. 44–45) is shedding.

Brain case (cranium)

Large orbit for eye

Upper jaw

Ear bone

Side view of skull of Japanese chin

Canine tooth

Lower jaw

Huge head

**DOGS' ANCESTOR**
Wolves (pp. 22–23) have typical long heads and muzzles.

**A JAPANESE CHIN**
All dogs are descended from wolves, even this Japanese chin, or spaniel, with its little round head and short curved jaws.

Orbit for eye

Upper molar

Canine tooth

Incisor

Hard palate

Ear bone

Zygomatic arch, or bony arch at outside edge of eye socket

Palatal view (showing roof of mouth) of skull of Japanese chin

Arctic wolf

Powerful nose

**DOG SLEUTH**
The bloodhound has a straight head, but not a pronounced muzzle; it uses its powerful sense of smell for tracking (pp. 16–17).

Palatal view of bat-eared fox

Small molar for eating insects

Bloodhound

Straight profile to head

Incisor

Hard palate

Fox terrier

**DIFFERENT TEETH**
The bat-eared fox has teeth that are different from any other canid (they are smaller, and there are 4 to 8 more than the usual 42) but its head is still doglike.

**STRAIGHT-LACED**
The fox terrier (pp. 52–53) has been bred to have a very straight head, with no angle between the brain case and the face.

Brain case (cranium)

Zygomatic arch of eye socket

Nasal region

Pekingese

Flat face

Ear bone

Incisor

Canine tooth

Side view of skull of bat-eared fox

Lower jaw

**PERKY PEKE**
Years of selective breeding (pp. 58–59) have given the Pekingese a small, round head, flat face, floppy ears, and soft fur.

13

# Sight and sound

Every domestic dog in the world, whether it is a Pekingese (pp. 58–59) or a Great Dane (pp. 56–57), has inherited the eyes and ears of its wild ancestor, the wolf. All its senses have evolved for being a social hunter of large prey, but these senses have been adapted and developed in different breeds of dog by "artificial selection." This means, for example, that in sight hounds (pp. 48–49), such as greyhounds, puppies with particularly good sight have been chosen over the centuries as future breeders. These breeders then pass on the trait of good sight to their puppies. So in the course of time, greyhounds have developed even better sight than the wolf. Wolves and domestic dogs cannot hear as well as some other carnivores, because they usually hunt at dusk when sight is more important than hearing. Foxes, however, hunt at night, and it is thought that their sense of hearing is more acute than a wolf's.

**HUNTING HORN**
Hunting dogs are trained to follow the sound of a horn as well as the human voice.

**DOG'S WHISTLE**
Most dogs will respond to the sound of a whistle.

**LISTENING DOG**
The large erect ears are turned this way and that as this dog works out where the sounds it is listening to are coming from.

Dense fur keeps the fennec warm on cold nights in the desert

**FENNEC FOX**
The fennec is the smallest member of the fox family. It lives in the Sahara and Arabian deserts and is well adapted for keeping cool and finding any food it can in the hot, dry sand.

The fennec's light-colored fur is pale to reflect the heat of the desert during the day

The fennec's huge ears allow body heat to escape, which helps to keep the animal cool in the hot desert

The belly fur is even paler, to reflect the heat from the ground

Outer ear

Ear muscle

Furry outside of ear

Brain

Bones of the inner ear

Ear canal

Ear cavity of skull

Glands

**THE EAR**
All wild members of the dog family have erect ears which help them to tell where a sound has come from.

### BEAUTIFUL BORZOI
The borzoi (pp. 46–47) is a typical sight hound, or gazehound. Because of its keen sight it was used in the Middle East for game hunting, and later by Russian royalty in traditional wolf hunts.

*The eyes are large and face forward so the borzoi probably has stereoscopic vision, which means that it can see in three dimensions, as humans do*

*Upper eyelid*

*Pupil*

*Iris*

*Lower eyelid*

*Third eyelid, or nictitating membrane*

### THE EYE
Inside a dog's upper and lower eyelids, there is a third eyelid – which protects the eye from dirt and dust.

*Muzzles (pp. 46–47) are usually worn by racing greyhounds*

### JACKAL-HEADED GOD OF MUMMIFICATION
Anubis, a jackal-headed god in ancient Egypt, supervised embalming and weighed the hearts of the dead.

*When the upper teeth closely overlap the lower teeth, it is called a scissor bite*

### A WINNING GREYHOUND
This greyhound is waiting intently for the start of the race, and all its senses are directed forward. As it races it will keep its eyes centered on the mechanical hare as though it were a live animal.

### MANED WOLF
The so-called "maned wolf" (pp. 32–33) of the South American savanna has very large ears for hearing the slightest sound in the long grass.

*Dog collar*

### THE CHASE IS ON
This pack of African hunting dogs is chasing a gemsbok. They use their big eyes to see their prey and their large ears to hear the communicating sounds of the pack, and also to hear whether any other predators are trying to take over their prey.

### GUARD DOG
This dog – an ancient Roman sculpture – is anxiously watching and listening for any thieves at the door.

# On the scent trail

POINTER POINTING
The pointer ranges over the
ground with its keen nose
and then "points" to
where the game is.

ALL MEMBERS OF THE CANID OR DOG FAMILY have a
far better sense of smell than any human, and they
probably remember scents better than sights. That is to say,
whereas humans remember how objects are placed in a room and
what they look like, a dog will remember the arrangement of the
objects by their different scents. In all wild canids – wolves, wild
dogs, jackals, and foxes – smell is the most highly developed
of all the senses. The animal hunts with its nose, finds its
mate with its nose, and identifies every new being that
comes into its territory with its nose. It can even tell
whether other animals are relaxed or afraid by their
smell. This intense perception of scent is made possible by the long nose of the skull, which contains
rolls of very thin bone over which the particles of
scent are drawn. With certain hunting and gun
dogs, there has been selection for the sense of
smell in preference to the other senses. These
dogs, such as the bloodhound, can smell very
well but are nearsighted.

**WHO ARE YOU?**
A dog can learn a lot
about another dog
by smelling the
anal gland just
beneath its tail.

*Drop ears in
scent hounds –
such as the beagle
– mean that their
hearing is not as
good as that of a
wild dog or fox,
with erect ears*

Saluki

Dalmatian

**TRUFFLE HUNTING**
A truffle is a fungus that
grows underground
and is considered to
be a great food
delicacy, especially
in France, where
dogs are trained to
search for truffles
by their smell.

*A nose, close to the ground,
picks up the scents of prey*

## ATTACKING
A fox would not usually attack a sheep, but it might do so if it could smell that the sheep was already dying.

**Nasal cavity with paper-thin turbinal bones**

**Sinuses**

**Cavity of brain**

**Fleshy nose**

**Lip**

**Palate**

## NASAL CAVITY
A dog's keen sense of smell is due to rolls of very fine bone, or turbinals, in its nasal cavity. These are connected to a fine mesh of nerve endings attached to the olfactory nerve, which takes scent messages to the brain.

## MINI DACHSHUND'S NOSE
Like all of the dog family, this miniature dachshund has a leathery nose and two nostrils through which scents are drawn into the nasal cavity.

*The bat-eared fox's keen sense of smell allows it to find its prey quickly*

## BAT-EARED FOX
The bat-eared fox eats any small animal or fruit that it can find, and it needs a keen sense of smell to look for beetles underground.

*Strong legs and excellent stamina make the beagle a dependable hunter*

## BEAGLE
Scent hounds, like this beagle, have been bred to use their noses more than their eyes and ears in the hunt. Because of this well-developed sense of smell, they can pursue small game very successfully. And with less keen hearing, the dog can concentrate on tracking a scent without being distracted by slight noises.

Looking for prey . . .

. . . and finding a surprise

## ENGLISH SETTER
Like the pointer, the setters are scent hounds. They are trained to "set up" game birds from the ground so they can be shot in the air.

# Behavior

Ears back show dog is afraid – or even potentially aggressive

Dog appears happy and relaxed – with pert ears and smiling mouth

Crossbred dog

THE DOG FAMILY can be divided into two distinct groups according to behavior: solitary hunters and social hunters. The solitary hunters – that is, the foxes and South American wild dogs (pp. 28–33) – live on their own, except when they are mating and rearing their young. The wolf, jackal, coyote, African hunting dog, dhole (pp. 22–27), and the domestic dog (pp. 14–17) are all social hunters. Their behavior is in many ways like that of a human family in which the parents are the leaders and the children do as they are told until they are old enough to leave and form their own family groups. In a wolf pack, or a family of African hunting dogs, every individual knows which other dog is above or below it in the family hierarchy, and it will fight hard to keep or to better its position. Even though wolves are such powerful killers, fights between them seldom end in death, and if one wolf is injured the others will often help it to feed.

**GETTING TO KNOW YOU**
The strong, dominant wolf on the left is greeting the weaker, more submissive wolf on the right.

*Ears laid back show fear or aggression*

*Tail between legs shows dog in a submissive stance*

*Mouth shut tightly denotes apprehension*

German shepherd

**BODY LANGUAGE**
Even though dogs cannot speak like humans, they say all they need to each other by the postures of their bodies and tails.

**JUST GOOD FRIENDS**
This charming painting by English artist John Charlton (1849–1917) shows three dogs of indistinct breeds (pp. 60–61) playing together in the snow and exhibiting their friendly relationship with one another.

*Crouched body means fox is waiting to pounce*

*Alert ears show fox is listening for potential prey*

## Solitary hunters

Foxes, including this American gray fox (pp. 28–29), are solitary hunters that kill their prey by themselves. They do not, therefore, have the complicated interactive behavior of the social hunters. A fox's tail cannot wag as expressively as a wolf's, and its upright ears are not as mobile. Even so, if a fox is frightened it will cower down to make itself look small, and if it is angry it will stand up as tall as it can to look large and threatening.

Gray tree-climbing fox

# Social hunters

The African hunting dog and other social hunters not only have to provide enough meat for the family group but they must also compete for food with, and defend themselves against, other large predators, like lions and hyenas. Human hunters have always been the main competitors of social hunters. The wolf (pp. 22–23) has been exterminated over much of its vast range in Europe and Asia, and the African hunting dog and the dhole (pp. 26–27) are also near extinction. Only jackals and the coyote (pp. 24–25), being smaller and more adaptable, continue to flourish.

Two wolves fighting it out to see which one will be the leader

**HOWLIN' WOLVES**
Like its wolf ancestors, this pointer will howl if left on its own in an effort to communicate with others of its kind. Some dogs will also howl when they hear certain kinds of music or, if they are kept outside, when the moon is full.

**TOP DOG**
Although much smaller than the Dalmatian, this Norfolk terrier has the stronger personality and is showing that he is top dog.

*Dalmatian's head is slightly turned away, showing fear*

*Norfolk terrier's positive stance shows his confidence toward the larger dog*

Dalmatian

Norfolk terrier

**FIGHTING FOR A BITE**
At a kill, these African hunting dogs will eat vast quantities of meat, which is later regurgitated, or vomited up, for their young, or for other members of the pack, who will fight over the half-digested morsels.

Pointer

**DOGS' SOCIAL CLUB**
This caricature by J. J. Granville, published in Paris, France, in 1859, emphasizes the similarity of dog behavior with that of humans.

# Cubs and puppies

T HE PUPPIES AND CUBS of all members of the dog family (Canidae) look similar when they are new-born. They are small, defenseless, and blind, and have short hair, short legs, and a little tail. At first, like all mammals, the cubs or puppies, which may vary in number from one to twelve or more, can only suck milk from their mother's nipples. After a few days (about nine for a domestic dog) their eyes open, they begin to hear, and they soon need more solid food. This is provided by the mother, and in social species by other members of the group, who re-gurgitate (vomit up) meat that they have previously eaten. A mother dog who looks as though she is being sick in front of her puppies is not ill but rather is providing them with their first solid meal. In the wild the young are nearly always born in a den or hole in the ground, and in the same way, a domestic dog needs a dark, warm place where she can give birth, which will happen about 63 days after she has been mated.

**FOOD FOR THOUGHT**
This mother fox is bringing home a rabbit for her three cubs, who are hungrily awaiting food in their den.

Four-week-old Great Dane puppies . . .

. . . playfully attacking each other . . .

**IT'S PLAYTIME**
It is essential that all puppies be allowed space in which to play. They must have exercise in order to grow properly, but of equal importance is their need to learn social interaction with other dogs and with humans. In this playing sequence, two Great Dane puppies (four weeks old) are learning to relate to each other.

. . . with one trying to dominate the other

All is well – they're friends again

**LOOKING ENDEARING**
The puppies of a Great Dane (above and right) are no dif-ferent in their needs from a Pekingese or a wolf. But, as they are the giants among dogs, they require a great deal of wholesome meat, extra calcium and vitamins, and large bones to chew (pp. 62–63). They also need plenty of space in which to play and exercise their growing limbs.

Six-week-old
Great Dane puppies

**NURSING MOTHER**
This mother wolf is contentedly suckling her cubs, but in a few weeks their sharp little milk teeth will have grown and will hurt her nipples. Then she will begin to wean the cubs with regurgitated meat.

**LEARNING TO BEHAVE**
The play of these African hunting dog pups is a school for adult life in which they must be powerful hunters. Just as with the Great Dane puppies, they learn the rules of social behavior from their games.

A small bronze Greek sculpture of a pregnant female – from the fifth century B.C.

Four-and-a-half-month-old black Labrador puppy

Dalmatian at six months

**A TAIL OF TWO PUPPIES**
These puppies are play fighting. The Dalmatian is a little older than the black Labrador retriever and is the dominant dog. Both of them are about half-grown, and in a few months they could be fighting in earnest.

**GETTING CARRIED AWAY**
All members of the dog family will carry their cubs around. Usually, it is the mother, but sometimes the father will also take the cub gently by the scruff of its neck with his teeth and carry it to safety.

**WOLF-BOYS**
Legend has it that the city of Rome in Italy was founded in 753 B.C. by two brothers – Romulus and Remus – who had been suckled as babies by a she-wolf.

# Leader of the pack

THE WOLF PACK is similar to a human family group, in which the oldest male and the oldest female are the leaders, and the young must do as they are told. Wolves and humans have many patterns of social behavior in common, for both evolved as social hunters who had to work together in a team so they could kill animals larger than themselves. Wolves guard their territory closely and make their presence known by howling (pp. 18–19). Each member of the pack knows his or her position in the scale of dominance, and any wolf that tries to assert itself is likely to be expelled from the pack by the leaders. The only pair of wolves to mate are the dominant male and the dominant female, and after the cubs are born the father will bring meat back to the den for the mother. The cubs are suckled for about 10 weeks; the mother and the younger wolves will feed them with regurgitated meat (partly digested meat returned to the mouth from the stomach) until they are old enough to hunt with the pack. At first, the young cubs can behave as they like and all the wolves will put up with their play fights, but as they grow older they too must learn to keep their place.

*Ears are erect to show that the wolf is on the alert – either for prey or foe*

**EUROPEAN GRAY WOLF**
In earlier times there were wolves in every country in Europe, but these wonderfully intelligent animals have been slaughtered by farmers and hunters for hundreds of years and they are now found only in limited quantities in southern and eastern Europe.

*Sharp teeth enable wolf to kill its prey quickly*

**A WOLF OF MANY COLORS**
The Arctic wolf from the far north of Canada has a hard life trying to find prey in the freezing cold of the Arctic. These wolves have a very thick white winter coat to camouflage them in the snow and ice, although during the summer they can be shades of gray or buff, or occasionally even black. They have short tails and small ears to keep the body as compact as possible. Arctic wolves feed on hares and birds, and sometimes, if they are lucky, a pack will be able to kill a deer or a musk ox.

**LITTLE RED RIDING HOOD**
When there really were wolves in the forests, mothers would have told their children the story of Little Red Riding Hood – of how she was tricked by a very clever wolf – to frighten them from going out alone.

**A RARE RED WOLF**
The red wolf is smaller than the gray wolf and is adapted for living in the warmer climate of the southeastern U.S. It was extinct in the wild, but in 1988 a few were reintroduced into North Carolina.

**WINNER OR LOSER**
Wolves are quick to snarl at each other, and they fight fairly often. But although a wolf can be seriously hurt in a fight, seldom will it be killed.

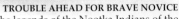

**TROUBLE AHEAD FOR BRAVE NOVICE**
According to the legends of the Nootka Indians of the Northwest, novices were sometimes carried away by wolves. This club may have been used as a display object to represent the powers the brave received during his captivity. It is made of abalone shell, bone, and human hair, and a wolf's head is carved at one end.

**TERROR OF WEREWOLVES**
According to folklore, a werewolf is a person who has changed into a wolf, or is capable of taking the shape of a wolf, while keeping its human intelligence. Many horror films have been made about werewolves.

*The legs have to be long and very powerful so the wolf can range over huge distances in search of prey*

**MAKING A MEAL OF IT**
A pack of wolves chase musk oxen on Ellesmere Island in the Arctic in the hope of finding food.

*The tail of this wolf is pointing down, showing it is wary of what is ahead*

23

# Jackals and coyotes

Limestone stele of Egyptian kneeling before the jackal of Wepwawet, with 63 other jackals, made after 550 B.C.

JACKALS, AND THE COYOTE, which lives only in North America, come below the wolf in the scale of social hunters (pp. 18–19) – the wolf being the most social of all animals that hunt on land. There are four species of jackals, all of which are found in Africa. The most widespread is the golden jackal, which is found in southeastern Europe and southern Asia as well as in Africa. Both the side-striped jackal and the black-backed jackal are found in Africa, south of the Sahara. The fourth jackal, the Simien jackal, lives only on the high plains of the Simen Mountains in Ethiopia, in the eastern part of Africa, and it is now in danger of extinction (pp. 12–13). All species of jackals, and the coyote, live in close-knit family groups which forage for any food they can find. Meals may vary from the carcass of an animal long since dead and left unwanted by other carnivores, to an antelope that the canids themselves have managed to kill. When a litter of pups is born (pp. 20–21), all the jackals in the family will help to look after them and bring back food for them to the den.

**A FIERCE FACE**
The Toltecs of Mexico worshiped a serpent god, Quetzalcoatl, shown here wearing a coyote headdress. It was found at a ruined palace in Tula, Mexico, and was made of shell and wood, between the seventh and ninth centuries A.D.

**GOLDEN OLDIES**
This pair of golden jackals will stay together for their whole lives, hunting and breeding together, unless one of them is killed. They will patrol their territory together, scent mark it with their urine, and prevent any intruding jackals from coming near.

**SILVER SADDLE**
The black-backed jackal has a spectacular coat of fine fur with a silver and black saddle. It lives on open grasslands in eastern and southern Africa.

This mummified canid in the form of the jackal god, Anubis, is from ancient Egypt (pp. 14-15), between 600 B.C. and A.D. 300

24

### SOCIAL COYOTE
The name "coyote" comes from the Aztec word, *coyotl*. The coyote – also called a brush, or prairie, wolf – is the jackal of North America and, like the jackal, it is a social hunter (pp. 18–19) that lives in pairs and family groups.

### CUNNING COYDOG
Wild coyotes sometimes mate with domestic dogs and produce "coydog" pups. As they are neither wild nor tame, coydogs have a hard time and often take to killing domestic livestock for food.

*Skull is smaller than a wolf's and has a flat forehead and comparatively small teeth*

*Golden jackal's coarse, short-haired coat varies in color from pale golden brown to brown-tipped yellow, depending on season and region*

### CANID QUICKSTEP
This golden jackal is doing a quick turn in its lookout for prey.

### DOG DANCE
Dogs were highly regarded by native North Americans, both for their meat and for transportation (pp. 56–57). This painting by the Swiss artist Karl Bodmer (1809–1893) shows a medicine man of the Hidatsa tribe wearing a special costume and performing a "dog dance." The Hidatsa tribe lived along the Missouri River in North Dakota.

### ETHIOPIAN HOWLER
The Simien jackal is in danger of extinction (pp. 12–13) because more and more of the high grassland plains where it lives are being taken over by farmers for livestock grazing. There may be only about 500 of these distinctive, tawny-red coated jackals left in the wild.

### JACKAL WORSHIP
Anubis, the jackal god, is frequently shown in ancient Egyptian artifacts.

# African and Asian dogs

THERE ARE MANY WILD CANIDS, aside from jackals (pp. 24–25) and wolves (pp. 22–23), living in Africa and Asia. In Africa there is the hunting dog (pp. 6–7) and the bat-eared fox (pp. 14–17) – which is not really a fox and has teeth that are different from those of all other wild dogs. In India and Southeast Asia there is the dhole, or red dog, as well as the raccoon dog, which comes from eastern Asia and Japan. All these wild dogs are social hunters. The Tibetan fox, from the high mountains of Tibet, and the Bengal fox are true foxes (pp. 28–29) and are solitary hunters (pp. 18–19) of small animals. Each of the many species of wild dog that lives in Asia and Africa is a carnivore with a specialized way of life that has evolved, or changed over many years. Each fills an ecological niche, or well-defined place, among the plants and other animals in its environment. Each wild dog or fox hunts its prey but is also hunted by other predators in its surroundings. In this way the population of any one group of animals does not grow too large, and the balance of nature is maintained.

**SOUTHERN SOLITAIRE**
The Cape fox of South Africa is the most southern of the true foxes. It is a small solitary hunter (pp. 18–19) with a silvery coat. The Cape fox lives in dry places and hunts at dusk.

**A MOST SOCIABLE DOG**
The African hunting dog is one of the most social of all members of the dog family. However, it is not a true dog, or canid (because it did not descend from the wolf); it belongs in a group of its own, the genus *Lycaon*. These dogs live in large family packs on grasslands and have an elaborate system of communication by means of body movements and sounds. Hunting by day, they range over a huge area in search of prey. They are vulnerable to disease and parasites, to other hungry carnivores (such as lions), and to human hunters.

*Large, rounded ears*

*Short, broad face and muzzle*

*Thin but well-muscled legs*

*Unique coat pattern is tan and gray with large white blotches*

*Having only four toes on the front foot makes the hunting dog unique among the dog family*

*White tuft at the end of the short bushy tail acts as a flag*

African hunting dog

Bat-eared fox

*Very large ears, up to 5 in (12 cm) long*

*Dark gray to black on face mask and muzzle*

**ENOUGH TEETH**
The bat-eared fox (pp. 16–17) has 46 to 50 teeth – compared to 42 in other species of canid. It feeds mostly on insects but will also eat fruits.

*Very long tail – up to 13 in (34 cm) in length*

**TWO-HEADED FETISH**
This *Konde*, or dog-shaped medicine figure, from Bakongo in Zaire, Africa, is used by driving nails into its wooden body to activate the magical healing forces within.

### INDIAN OR CHINESE?
The dhole, or red dog, is a social hunter (pp. 18–19) with some characteristics like the African hunting dog, although apart from the rounded ears, they do not look at all alike. Neither of these canids will interbreed with domestic dogs. The Chinese dhole has a thicker, darker coat than the more southern Indian dhole.

*Rounded ears*

*Dark red coat*

*Long, bushy tail*

Chinese dhole

*Tawny-colored coat*

Indian dhole

*Tail is darker color than rest of coat*

### ON TOP OF THE WORLD
The Tibetan fox lives on the high, icy-cold plateaus of Tibet above 12,000 ft (4,000 m). It has a very thick, furry coat to keep it warm and long, slender jaws for pulling small rodents out of their burrows.

*Tail is short, relative to its body length*

*White variety of coat shows this dog has been bred in captivity for its fur*

*Short, sharply pointed muzzle*

Raccoon dog in winter coat

### WHEN IS A RACCOON NOT A RACCOON?
The raccoon dog (above and right) has this name because it looks similar to a raccoon. It is a chubby canid with a short tail and a very thick, fine coat of gray-black and white fur. Because the coat is highly valued by fur traders (pp. 12–13), the raccoon dog has been bred in captivity in many countries. In the U.S.S.R., captive animals were allowed to go free and are now living as wild populations (pp. 36–37) which are spreading westward.

*Short, erect ears rounded at top*

### ONE LITTLE INDIAN
The Bengal fox is like a small red fox. It lives on open grasslands and scrub in India and digs its own dens. Like all foxes it hunts rodents, lizards, and other small animals.

*Black facial mask, like that of a true raccoon*

Raccoon dog in dark summer coat

*True raccoon of North and South America belongs to the Procyonidae family*

27

# Red fox, gray fox

ALL FOXES ARE SOLITARY HUNTERS that live on their own (pp. 18–19) – except in the mating season. They have long bodies, sharply pointed faces, and a bushy tail which is often called a "brush." Foxes have highly developed senses (pp. 14–17) and large, erect ears. Their usual prey are rodents and rabbits. The red fox is one of the most common carnivores in the world and is known to most people from fables and stories for its cunning. Besides the red fox there are nine other species in the fox group – or the genus *Vulpes* (pp. 26–27, 30–31). The gray fox of North and Central America belongs to another group – the genus *Urocyon*. It has different habits from the red fox and is noted for its ability to climb trees. The red fox is very adaptable and can live in many different environments from deserts and mountains to the centers of cities.

**THE QUACK FROG**
This is one of Greek storyteller Aesop's (620–560 B.C.) many fables. It tells the story of a frog who claimed to be a learned doctor. The fox asked him why, if he was so skilled, did he not heal his own strange walk and wrinkled skin.

**WAITING FOR LUNCH**
Fox cubs (pp. 20–21) will stay with their mother for several months before they must leave her and find their own territories.

**MAKING TRACKS**
The paw prints of a fox are smaller than those of most dogs – the marks of the pads are longer, and the claws are sharply pointed.

*Coat can range in color from grayish and rust-red to a flame red*

**FURRY BEAUTIFUL**
The red fox's fur is so beautiful that for thousands of years people have made clothes for themselves from their pelts. Captive foxes have also been bred for their furs in a variety of different coat colors. Nowadays, clothes made of animal furs are unacceptable to many people who care about animals (pp. 12–13).

*The tail of the red fox, which always has a white tip, does not express the animal's feelings the way the tail of a dog does*

## GETTING TO THE TOP

The gray tree fox is found in the United States (except in the Rocky Mountains and the Northwest), Central America, and northern South America. It is a little smaller than the red fox and has a salt-and-pepper coat with a reddish belly.

A gray tree-climbing fox on the lookout for prey, which can be rabbits, insects, or carrion (dead animals)

*Tip of the tail may be black, or grayish like the coat, but it is never white*

*Nose and sides of muzzle are black*

## A BIRD IN VIEW

The red fox (left) does not climb trees (whereas the gray fox spends much of its time in trees looking for birds and eggs to eat) – from a scene printed on an English Wedgwood plate, c.1764.

## A-HUNTING WE SHALL GO

In many countries fox hunting (pp. 14–15) is part of the sporting life of the country-side. Because they are such successful carnivores, foxes can become a pest to farmers by killing chickens and game birds. Hunting controls the numbers of foxes, but many people think it is cruel.

*Fox's acute sense of smell (pp. 16–17) encourages it to cover distances of up to 6 miles (10 km) in search of food*

*Throat and chin have white or light-colored fur*

## STREET-WISE

In some cities foxes are becoming increasingly common. They kill rats, scavenge for food from garbage cans, and even seem to learn road sense.

## BLACK OR RED?

American artist John James Audubon (1785–1851) painted a wide variety of wildlife, including the black, or melanistic, form of the red fox.

## DEEP IN THE FOREST

English artist William Morris (1834–1896), who designed this tapestry, had a great regard for the natural world. To him, as to many people today, the fox was an essential part of every woodland scene.

# Hot foxes, cold foxes

**HOT DOG!**
The hot dog, called a frankfurter in Europe, was first made in Germany during the Middle Ages.

NOT ALL SPECIES OF FOXES live in the temperate (moderate) parts of the world and feed off the abundant rats, mice, and small birds there. A few foxes live exceedingly harsh lives in the coldest – as well as in the hottest – lands. Only one fox lives in the icy cold Arctic regions of Alaska, Canada, northern Europe, and Asia, and that is the Arctic fox. Arctic foxes have been known to cover a territory of 15,000 acres (6,000 hectares) in their search for food; they have small ears, which cut down on heat loss, and dense fur, which keeps them warm in winter. There are also a number of different species of fox that live in the world's hottest deserts. Generally, very little food is available for these foxes, so they have evolved as hunters and scavengers; they range over huge areas in search of some food to keep them alive. Foxes that live in hot, dry deserts all have very large ears which help keep them cool, small bodies that can survive on little food, and short, dense fur. They sleep in dens, or hollows in the sand, during the intense heat of the day, and hunt by night when it can actually be very cold.

**DESERT FOX**
The fennec fox is the smallest of all the foxes, and it probably has the most difficult time of all in finding food. It lives in the parched Arabian and Sahara deserts where there are very few other animals, so food is always scarce.

*Soft, dense coat is designed to keep the Arctic fox warm and is thicker in winter*

*Short, furry ears cut down heat loss – in winter they must not become frostbitten*

*Dark brown and white summer coat*

*Adult's tail is very bushy, and can be as long as 12 in (30 cm)*

Arctic fox cub in dark summer coat

**COAT OF MANY COLORS** *above and right*
The Arctic fox can be seen here in four different colored coats. The fox on the right has the polar, or white, form of its winter coat and lives in the high Arctic where there is nearly always snow on the ground. In the summer, this fox will have a brown and white coat, as above. There is another less common variety of Arctic fox which is called "blue." The winter coat of the "blue" fox is steely gray, but in summer it is all brown. Shedding occurs twice a year – in spring and autumn – when it is time for a color change.

A pair of Arctic foxes – one in a dark summer coat, the other in a pale winter coat

*Hind foot has a thick covering of soft fur all over it – even under the pads*

*Big ears of the sand fox are typical of "hot foxes" – but they're not as big as those of the fennec*

**HALF A FENNEC FOX, HALF A RED FOX**
Often confused with the fennec, this small desert fox from North Africa and the Arabian Desert actually shares many characteristics with the red fox (pp. 28–29). Although its skull, teeth, and coloring are similar to the red fox's, this sand fox has a smaller body, is more delicately built, and has much bigger ears.

**A WHITER SHADE OF PALE**
The pale fox lives in grasslands at the southern edge of the Sahara Desert in Africa. Like the fennec, it is a small, pale-colored fox.

*Long bushy tail can be curled around the body to keep it warm during cold desert nights*

Rüppell's sand fox

**AFTER A MEAL**
The fennec must have sharp senses (pp. 14–15) and quick movements if it is to catch these jumping rodents.

*Thick ruff of very fine fur around the neck*

**SWIFTLY, SWIFTLY**
The kit, or swift, fox is the only desert fox in North America. Today, it is found only in the southwestern U.S. and Mexico. It used to be much more widespread until poisoned bait, meant for wolves and coyotes, also killed many kit foxes.

The kit fox lives in the deserts of North America

Adult Arctic fox in pale winter coat

*Thick fur on feet almost hides claws*

31

# South American mix

Stirrup cup – with a fox on man's forehead – from Mochica tribe of pre-Columbian Peru, A.D. 300–1000

**CULPEO'S COAT**
The culpeo's grayish yellow and black coat, with a black-tipped tail, is not in demand for making fur clothing (pp. 12–13), so this canid is not, at present, in danger of extermination.

SOUTH AMERICAN WILD DOGS are often referred to as foxes or zorros (the Spanish name for foxes), but they should not be confused with either true wolves (pp. 22–23) or true foxes (pp. 28–29). They are solitary hunters (pp. 18–19) of small animals, but they will also eat anything edible that they can find, including fruit. There are four distinct genera, or groups, of foxlike dogs: the short-legged bush dog; the maned wolf; at least six different members of the *Dusicyon* genus, of which the most common is the culpeo; and the doglike, crab-eating (or forest) zorro, which is in the *Cerdocyon* genus. This crab-eating zorro is sometimes tamed by the Indians and will go hunting with them like a domestic dog. Another zorro that used to live on South America's Falkland Islands until the late 1800s was exterminated by fur traders. Charles Darwin (1809–1882), English naturalist and author of *The Origin of Species*, visited the Falklands in 1834 on his voyage around the world in the ship HMS *Beagle*, and described this animal as the "Falkland Island wolf."

**PRETTY PATAGONIAN**
The Patagonian fox, or chilla, lives in the southern part of South America. Like many canids in the genus *Dusicyon*, it is not at all timid. In 1834, Darwin killed one by walking close and hitting it on the head with a hammer.

**HEAVILY HUNTED**
Found in the pampas of Argentina and southern Brazil, this gray-bodied, red-headed fox, or zorro, has a very long, bushy tail.

Azara's zorro

Bush dog

*Small ears*

*Broad face*

*Reddish tan, or tawny, coat*

*Very short legs*

**BUSH BADGER**
The bush dog looks more like an otter or badger than a dog. Like other South American members of the dog family, this animal is not a true dog or fox, but belongs in a group – the genus *Speothos* – on its own. It is found in open country near water in tropical South America and spends much of its time in a burrow.

*Large, erect ears with white fur inside*

*Erect mane with darker fur running down nape of neck and back*

**A DOG OF LITTLE EARS**
The small-eared dog, or zorro, is one of the rarest of the South American dog family. It lives in the tropical rain forests, but nothing is known of its habits.

*Dark muzzle*

**MAGNIFICENT MANE**
The maned wolf – in the genus *Chrysocyon* – is different from all other members of the dog family in that its tail is very short and its legs are longer than the length of its body. This animal is not a wolf and it is not a fox, though it is sometimes called the "stilt-legged fox." The maned wolf lives in the tall grass and woodlands of southern Brazil and hunts by pouncing on small animals.

Maned wolf

*Very long, stilt-like legs*

*Reddish yellow coat*

Maned wolf's short, bushy tail has mostly white fur at its tip

Nazca pottery fox from coast of Peru, 500 B.C. – A.D. 600

**THE CRAB-EATING ZORRO**
This brindled gray, crab-eating fox probably does not often eat crabs, so forest fox is a better name. It is a doglike creature and lives in the tropical forests of northeastern South America.

*Dark-colored fur on legs and feet make it look as if it is wearing stockings*

# Early domestication

Egyptian papyrus, c.1500–1200 B.C., showing two jackals and some goats

THE WOLF IS THE ANCESTOR of all domestic dogs (pp. 48–61), including the Irish wolfhound, which is much larger than the wolf, and the Pekingese, which is very much smaller. The outward appearance of these breeds may look completely different from the wolf and from each other, but every dog, inside its skin, feels and behaves like a wolf. Humans probably first began to live closely with tamed wolves during the last Ice Age, more than 12,000 years ago, and the bones of these early dogs are sometimes found on archeological sites. The people of ancient Egypt and western Asia were the first to begin breeding distinctive kinds of dogs such as mastiffs and greyhounds. Most of the different shapes and sizes of dogs known today were already in existence by the first century B.C. This is known from the skeletal remains of these dogs, but more especially from models, paintings, and other works of art which often portray the animals in marvelous detail. In the ancient world, dogs were kept for hunting, herding, protection (pp. 40–45), sport (pp. 46–47), and, as today, companionship.

**JACKAL GOD**
The jackal has always had a close association with humans, though it is not an ancestor of the domestic dog. Anubis, the jackal god, was a most important ancient Egyptian deity (god). This one is made of limestone, A.D. 300.

**PERSIAN PLAQUE**
This stylized half-dog, half-bird – or "fenmurv" – is a fertility symbol. It is made of silver, c.7th century A.D., sometime during the Sassanid dynasty, and was found in northern India.

*Handle decorated with coral*

**FRENCH FLAGON**
This Celtic drinking vessel, made of bronze, c.400 B.C., was found near Basse-Yutz in France. Along the handle, two hounds chase a duck which seems to be swimming when liquid is poured.

**ANCIENT HUNTSMEN**
Assyrian huntsmen walk with their mastiff-like hounds in a royal park in this bas-relief from a palace at Nineveh, the ancient capital of Assyria, built between 645–635 B.C.

## EASTERN WORSHIP

In the Far East, dogs are used for many purposes and the images of dogs are included in religious worship. This stone temple god, in the form of a lionlike dog, is from Thailand.

## GREEK URN

This beautiful vase is of Greek design (c.380–360 B.C.), though it was found in southern Italy. The young girl is dangling a tortoise to tease her pet dog. The bracelets on her ankle are to ward off evil spirits.

The Townley hounds sculpture, collected by the Englishman Charles Townley (1737–1805), was found at Monte Cagnolo near Rome, Italy, during the late 1700s

## ONE WOMAN AND HER DOG

This is the skeleton of a woman who was buried with her hand resting on the body of her dog. The skeletons were found in Israel on an archeological site called Ein Mallaha and date back to about 12,000 years ago. This is one of the earliest examples of a domestic dog ever to be discovered in the world.

## TOWNLEY HOUNDS

The Romans kept dogs from the earliest times. They used greyhounds and bloodhounds for hunting; large mastiffs were thought of as ideal not only as fighting dogs but also in war. This exquisite marble sculpture from Rome, 2nd century A.D., is of a pair of seated greyhounds.

## DOGS' COLLARS

Dogs have been wearing collars ever since Egyptian times. We know this because dogs in art have been depicted wearing collars – from a painting found in Pompeii to relatively modern paintings and sculptures.

Italian brass collar

German spiked iron collar

## CAVE CANEM

Just as today "Beware of the dog" is written on gates, the Romans wrote *Cave canem*, which means the same in Latin. This mosaic, c.4th century A.D., comes from an entrance hall of a villa, excavated in Bodrum in Turkey.

Silver presentation collar

## DOG ROSE

The ancient Greeks thought this flower had magical qualities and used it to treat people who had been bitten by a rabid dog (pp. 62–63).

Pottery vessel – from the Colima culture in Mexico, A.D. 300–900 – of a hairless "techichi" dog

# Feral dogs

AFTER THE FIRST DOGS were domesticated about 12,000 years ago, some of them, like the dingo, eventually reverted to life in the wild. They are known as "feral" dogs. They hunted for their own food except when they could scavenge for a few scraps left by human hunters. In many parts of the world, dogs still live like this. Many populations of dogs live and breed without any human contact at all. The most successful of all feral dogs is the dingo of Australia, but there are also feral dogs in India and many other parts of Asia, where they are called "pariah" dogs – "pariah" is a Tamil, or Sri Lankan, word meaning "outcast." All over Africa feral dogs live on the outskirts of villages, where they serve a useful function in cleaning up all the garbage. At times these dogs are allowed into the houses, but they are seldom given anything to eat because there is often not enough food for the people, let alone the animals. So the dogs must fend for themselves.

**FERRETING FOR FOOD**
The feral dogs of Egypt are sometimes lucky and find scraps of food left by tourists.

**IN THE WILDS OF INDIA**
Pariah dogs have been living wild in India for thousands of years. Some look like the dingoes of Australia.

**SANTO DOMINGO DOG**
This dog must have looked very similar to the wild dogs that Christopher Columbus (1451–1506) probably found in the West Indies when he discovered America.

**PERUVIAN PARIAH**
Long before the Spanish first went to South America, the native peoples had dogs that lived around the settlements, just as their descendants, the feral dogs of today, do.

**QUINKAN SPIRITS**
In these cave paintings near Cape York in Australia, these "Quinkan spirits" – the Great Ancestors of the aborigines – are accompanied by a dingo.

A sitting dingo

*Nose is used for sniffing prey, such as lizards, rabbits, or rodents, or even fruit and plants*

*Eye of a dingo is more like that of a wolf than a dog*

**DOMINANT DINGO**
These young dingoes know which one is the dominant dog.

## THE AUSTRALIAN DOG
The dingoes of Australia (above and right) have been so successful at living in the wild that it has only recently been recognized that they were originally domestic dogs taken to Australia by the native aborigines at least 4,000 years ago. Dingoes should be preserved as part of the unique animal kingdom of Australia because – except where they have interbred with European dogs – they are probably the only remaining purebred descendants of prehistoric domestic dogs.

**THE ARISTOCRAT OF DOGS**
The dingo, as depicted in this old engraving, is the aristocrat of all breeds. It is the most purebred dog in the world, because there are no other wild dogs with which it can breed.

**MOTHER AND BABIES**
Like all dogs, the dingo is descended from the wolf (pp. 22–23). Like the wolf, the dingo mates once a year and brings up its young to be social hunters (pp. 18–19).

*Coat is a tawny yellow with pale underparts*

*Dingo's feet are like a wolf's – there is no dewclaw (pp. 6–7) on the hind foot*

*Tail is long and bushy – sometimes with a white tip*

*Feet are white*

# Development of breeds

Elegant lurcher shows typical bone structure of a dog

MANY BREEDS OF DOGS are hundreds of years old, such as spaniels, greyhounds, and terriers, but a new breed can be developed at any time by crossing two or more different breeds. The Sealyham terrier is one example of a new breed of terrier (pp. 52–53) that was developed in the 1800s in Sealyham, Wales. It is also possible to reconstitute, or "remake," a breed that has become extinct. For example, the Irish wolfhound, which died out about a hundred years ago, was reconstituted as a new line from a cross of Great Danes, deerhounds, and mastiffs (pp. 48–49). Prior to the first dog show in England in 1859, there was considerable variation in the size, shape, and color of dogs within a single breed. Today, however, the dogs within one breed all look very similar because of the required standards for showing. Standardizing can be harmful to breeds, as the dogs lose their individual characteristics. It can also lead to inherited ailments and is why German shepherds are prone to dislocated hips.

**"YE OLDE MIMICKE DOGGE"**
In the late 1500s there was an imaginary beast called a "Mimicke Dogge." Some people thought it probably had a shaggy coat and was good at performing tricks like a poodle; others thought it had an "ape's wit and a hedgehog's face."

*The turned-up corners of the mouth make this lurcher look as if it is smiling*

**IT'S RAINING CATS, DOGS, AND PITCHFORKS**
This old English saying may be based on the ancient Chinese spirits for rain and wind, which were sometimes depicted as a cat and a dog. Here, the English caricaturist George Cruikshank (1792–1878) offers his interpretation.

Lurcher

**SECRET SYMBOLS**
American "kings of the road" – tramps, or hobos – used secret signs to let their friends know whether there was a dog (left), or a bad dog (below), on a stranger's property.

Dog

Bad dog

Wedgwood majolica (highly glazed earthenware) punch bowl, decorated with puppet Punch and his clown-dog Toby

## BULL'S-EYE

This bull terrier starred with Oliver Reed, who played Sikes in the 1968 film *Oliver!*, based on a novel by English writer Charles Dickens (1812–1870). Bull terriers were developed in the 1700s by crossing bulldogs and terrier types to produce a fierce fighting dog (pp. 46–47). Their small, fine, erect ears were developed to avoid illegal ear-cropping (pp. 44–45).

## A FIGHT TO THE FINISH

The Staffordshire bull terrier first entered the show ring as a recognized breed in 1935. It was developed in the Midlands of England, originally as a fighting dog, by crossing the old-fashioned bull terrier with the bulldog and the now-extinct Old English terrier.

*Small, half-pricked ears*

*Very muscular body*

Staffordshire bull terrier

## THE ROUGH AND THE SMOOTH

These popular terriers were first bred in the 1800s by Jack Russell, a clergyman from Devon, England. These small dogs were a cross between several now-extinct breeds and varied much in appearance and size. Kennel clubs are beginning to recognize the Jack Russell as an official breed – for example, the British Kennel Club made the Parson Jack Russell (but not all Jack Russells) an official breed in 1990, but in the U.S. and Canada the Jack Russell is still not recognized as an official breed for showing.

*V-shaped ears, falling forward*

*Dark, deep-set eyes*

*Coat can be long and rough-haired, or short and smooth-haired*

Jack Russell terriers

*Streamlined body and short-haired coat make a dog built for speed*

Thomas Bewick's (pp. 42–43) engraving of an old-fashioned lurcher

## IN THE LURCH

The lurcher was originally a crossbreed (pp. 60–61) between a greyhound and a terrier; its patience, intelligence, speed, and fighting ability made it a perfect dog for a poacher (pp. 40–41). Many owners would like to enter their lurchers in the show ring, but as yet they are still not recognized as an official breed.

## HEAD OVER HEELS

It's hard to say what breed this little dog is – but he has certainly surprised his mistress with his amusing antics.

# Hunting dogs

**HUNTING IN INDIA**
The Mogul emperors of India had just as many rituals of hunting as the feudal lords of medieval Europe. Akbar (1542–1605) is shown here hunting black buck, or Indian antelope, with Saluki-type hounds.

**MEDIEVAL HUNTING DOGS**
Medieval hunters usually had a pack of at least 12 running hounds and a well-trained scent hound, or lyam-hound, whose task was to frighten the game out of its hiding place. In this detail of a picture in *Benninck's Book of Hours*, the game is a wild boar.

FOR CENTURIES DOGS were used for hunting wild animals all over the world. In medieval times, hunting from horseback with dogs became an important part of life for the kings and feudal lords of Europe. Hunting was considered necessary as training for tournaments of chivalry and for warfare. The laws of hunting, or venery as it was called then, were very complicated; certain animals were preserved for only the nobility to hunt. Important "beasts of venery" were the red deer stag (male) and hind (female), the hare, wild boar, and wolf. The fallow deer, roe deer, fox, and wildcat were considered of secondary value and were called "beasts of the chase." Special breeds of scent and sight hounds (pp. 14–17) were used at different times during these hunts and were kept in royal kennels. The most valuable dogs were those trained to hunt large game.

**COME BLOW THE HORN**
Blowing the horn with a series of long and short notes was a very important part of the rituals of medieval hunting.

The Savernake Horn was made of ivory in 12th-century England. Hunting scenes engraved in silver were added in the 14th century

### THE THRILL OF THE CHASE
A horse, rider, and hunting dogs chase a stag along this French watch chain, beautifully crafted in silver and gold in 1845.

### GAMEKEEPER AND HIS DOGS
Many traditions connected with hunting and shooting remain unchanged since medieval times. The gamekeeper's job of protecting game from predators and poachers is still the same as it was when the laws of venery were first enacted in the 11th century.

### BENIN PIECE
The Benin bronzes from Nigeria are famous throughout the world for their great artistic value. This bronze plaque, made by a Nigerian artist in the late 16th century, is of a Portuguese soldier with his gun and hunting dog.

### RUNNING WITH THE PACK
This late 19th-century painting, by British artist Alfred Duke, shows a pack of hunting beagles picking up the scent and creating a noisy clamor. These bold, strong, intelligent dogs may have an ancient origin. The Norman French used them for pursuing hares – they were so small that they were carried in saddle-bags or the pockets of mounted hunters.

### SWIMMING DOG
This golden retriever has been told to fetch a stick out of the water, but it would collect a dead animal killed in a hunt just as quickly. Most dogs enjoy a swim, but retrievers are specially bred to bring back birds and other animals that have been shot and have fallen into the water. These dogs are trained to respond quickly to commands. They have a "soft" mouth, which means they can carry a dead bird in their mouths without biting into it. Their fur has a very thick, water-resistant undercoat.

### DIANA THE HUNTRESS
This enamel painting on a metal plaque from Limoges shows what hunting hounds looked like in France in the mid-16th century. The picture is of Diana, the Roman goddess of the hunt. There are many legends about Diana, who shunned the society of men and was attended always by a large number of nymphs. In classical art she was often shown in a chariot drawn by two white stags.

*All dogs swim by paddling with their front legs, just as children do when they are learning to swim by "dog-paddling"*

# Herding dogs and sheepdogs

THE USE OF DOGS TO PROTECT and herd livestock dates from as early as 1000 B.C., when farmers began to breed large numbers of sheep, goats, and cattle. In his book on raising farm animals, in the first century A.D., the Roman writer Columella noted that shepherds preferred white sheepdogs because they could be distinguished from wolves. There was always a danger that the shepherd would kill his own dog, believing it to be a wolf that was about to kill his animals. Even today, although the wolf is nearly extinct, most of the many varieties of herding dogs that are bred in nearly every country of the world are light-colored or tan and have a lot of white in their coats.

**LASSIE**
The rough collie got a new name from the *Lassie* films.

**OLD DOG'S TAIL**
Old English sheepdogs are seldom born without tails, and most puppies have their tails docked (pp. 44–45) for showing. A heavy sheepdog without a tail is not much use because it cannot run fast. Although called "Old," this breed is probably not of ancient origin. In this 19th-century English painting, the sheepdog is ready to tend its sheep.

**ROUGH COLLIE**
The original rough collie was the traditional sheepdog of the lowlands of Scotland, and probably took its name from the "colley," or local black sheep. For hundreds of years it was an essential partner for every shepherd. Today, the rough collie is one of the world's most popular breeds and has become a successful show and companion dog.

*Straight, muscular forelegs and powerful, sinewy hindlegs enabled the rough collie to cover great distances while herding sheep*

*Long-haired, thick coat is usually pale gold, tan, and white, with dark hair around the head*

**BELGIAN SHEPHERD DOG**
There were no wolves left in Belgium when the shepherd dogs of this country were first developed as distinct breeds in the 1880s. Therefore they, and indeed the modern German shepherd, are an exception to the tradition that herding dogs should be light-colored.

**ROUND-UP TIME**
The Border collie, originally from the border country between England and Scotland, is one of the finest sheepdogs in the world. It is bred as a working dog, not for showing.

**DOGS DOWN UNDER**
The Australian cattle dog is now the official name for this breed of strong working dog, developed by cattlemen in the 1830s. It has had a number of previous names, such as the Queensland blue heeler. These dogs round up cattle by nipping at their heels.

**A SHEPHERD AND HIS DOG**
Both this Rumanian shepherd and his dog
are well prepared for the rigors of the
winters in central Europe. These
traditional breeds – of both sheepdog
and shepherd – are heavily built,
have thick coats, and are excellent
guardians of the flock.

**IMPASSE**
Englishman Thomas Bewick (1753–1828) was
famous for his animal engravings. Here
a dog teases
a bull.

*The ears should be
semi-erect with the
tips pointing
forward*

**SMALL BUT BEAUTIFUL**
Domestic animals on the
Shetland Islands, off the
northern coast of Scotland, tend
to be small. This is because the
climate is cold and windy,
and food is often scarce.
So small animals, such
as the Shetland pony and
Shetland breed of cattle,
survive better in the
tough conditions than larger
animals that need more
food. The Shetland
sheepdog, or shelty,
is also a successful
product of breeding
for small size. A tiny
version of the
Scottish rough
collie, it was the
traditional herding dog
of the Shetland
Islands.

*The shelty's sharp
sense of smell can
seek out and save
a lamb that is
buried in the
snow*

# Helper dogs

To catch a thief

**DOGS OF WAR**
The intense loyalty of dogs to people means that they can be trained to carry out missions under conditions of great danger.

DOGS HAVE BEEN INDISPENSABLE throughout history as helpers in human societies. Besides being used to herd other animals, and for companionship, their principal function has been to guard the home and the farm. Today the job of the guard dog has broadened and includes protecting factories and industrial estates. To shut up a dog on its own in an empty building or other enclosed space and expect it to live by itself, and to ward off intruders, goes against all the social behavioral patterns of the dog, and is cruel. Dogs that are trained by the police for protection and for detection of drugs and explosives are seldom alone and usually live well-balanced lives. Certain breeds are more naturally aggressive than others, but nearly all dogs have to be specially trained to be aggressive to strangers and not to their handlers. Today there are innumerable ways in which dogs help the sick, the disabled, and the lonely – and by insisting on a daily walk they help keep their owners healthy.

*Strong teeth and a sturdy jaw – with the lower jaw projecting above the upper – help the boxer to keep strangers at bay*

Boxers have great strength and energy – the powerful forequarters are inherited from the bulldog

*Thick black and tan coat is long and wavy and provides perfect protection against the intense cold of the Swiss mountains*

**BERNESE MOUNTAIN DOG**
In the old days the large mastiff-type dogs in Switzerland were used for protecting merchants, cattle traders, drovers, and their herds as they traveled through the mountain passes. Until the early 1900s they were all known simply as Swiss mountain dogs, but today there are four separate breeds – the Bernese (pp. 56–57) from the province, or canton, of Berne; the Appenzell from the canton of the same name; the Entlebuch from the canton of Lucerne; and the Greater Swiss.

**DOGS IN SPACE**
Sending dogs into space may have contributed greatly to human knowledge, but for the dogs it must have been a terrifying experience – no different from any other laboratory experiment. The first dog to be sent into space was the Russian dog Laika in 1957.

St. Bernard to the rescue

**RESCUE DOGS**
For several hundred years, dogs bred at the monastery of the Great St. Bernard Pass in Switzerland were trained to rescue travelers lost in the mountains.

**A DOG WITH THREE HEADS**
In ancient mythology, Cerberus was a three-headed dog that stood at the gates of hell, to prevent the living from entering and the dead from leaving.

БЕЛКА и СТРЕЛКА

German shepherds have plenty of room in their straight, wolflike jaws for strong, healthy teeth

## SEEING EYE DOGS
Most people know that dogs can be trained to be "the eyes" of people who are blind. They can also learn to hear for the deaf, be a helping hand to disabled people, and provide companionship to the old, the sick, and the deprived.

*Cutting the ears to make them permanently erect (cropping) is illegal in Britain, but it is done in other countries to make the dog look fiercer*

*Cutting off the tail (docking) is a painful procedure and prevents the dog from expressing its natural behavior*

This Doberman pinscher is warning an intruder not to come any closer

## THE FIERCE DOBERMAN
The Doberman pinscher is a born guard dog and has been bred to be aggressive. But like nearly all dogs, when correctly reared, it can also be an affectionate companion. The breed was first developed in Germany at the end of the 19th century.

## GOOD COMPANIONS
Both the boxer and the German shepherd (pp. 10–11) are guard dogs and were first bred in Germany. The boxer is of mastiff origin (pp. 34–35) crossed with the bulldog (pp. 54–55). The German shepherd is a droving or herding dog that has become the most popular guardian and protector of property worldwide. Dogs of both breeds are also loyal and affectionate companions for people if reared and trained correctly, but they need plenty of space and exercise.

*The powerful hindquarters make the German shepherd a good jumper and able to cover great distances without getting tired*

## BRAVE GUARD DOG
As long as this dog can spend most of its time with a person, it will be content and can be trained to protect and guard people and buildings.

45

# Dogs in sports

OVER THE AGES, people have used dogs as entertainment in a great variety of sports, many of which have unfortunately involved much cruelty. In Roman times, dogfighting and "baiting" became fashionable sports and continued until the late 1800s. Baiting was a sport in which people released a pack of dogs in a ring with another animal, such as a bear or bull (pp. 54–55), and watched as the animal was torn to death by the dogs. Although these inhumane activities are now illegal, they are still practiced in some places. Dogs like to compete with each other, however, and there are many sports that are not as cruel. The large number of different breeds of sight hounds (pp. 14–15) have all been developed for coursing, or chasing after, fast-running prey such as hares. They were often used – together with birds of prey – in the sport of falconry. In northern Africa and Asia, both the Saluki and the Afghan hound (pp. 48–49) were bred for chasing gazelles. Today, in greyhound racing, dogs are bred for speed, and run after a mechanical "hare."

**GOING TO THE DOGS**
Greyhounds and whippets are the number-one choice around the world as racing dogs. Here, though, the greyhound is used for advertising Camembert cheese.

**"THE DOG FIGHT"**
The spectators in this painting, by English artist Thomas Rowlandson (1756–1827), are urging their dogs to fight and are betting on which dog will win. Today this cruel sport is illegal in the U.S. and many other countries.

*Keen sight of the borzoi (pp. 14–15) will help it to win a race – or, as in former times, to hunt well*

**MUZZLED**
Dogs get very excited when they are racing, so usually they wear muzzles to keep them from biting other dogs during a race.

Borzoi

*Deep chest and freely swinging shoulders enable the dog to take long strides*

*Long, muscular lower legs*

*Well-feathered tail is long, set low, and gently curved*

Well-muscled legs make the Saluki a powerful runner

### THE ROYAL SALUKI
The Saluki is one of the oldest breeds of sight hound (pp. 14–15) in the world, and dogs of this type can be seen in the tomb paintings of ancient Egyptian pharaohs. For thousands of years Salukis have been bred by Arab peoples for chasing gazelles and, together with falcons, for killing large birds, such as vultures.

### AWAY TO THE RACES
Although dogs have been used in the Arctic for hundreds of years to draw sleds (pp. 56–57), today they have been mostly replaced by mechanical snowmobiles. However, within recent years, the sport of sled racing over long distances with huskies has become very popular – especially in Alaska.

### TINTIN AND SNOWY
These popular cartoon characters race over the snow with their trusty team of huskies.

*Dense, curly ruff on neck*

*Long, wavy, silky hair is usually white with splotchy dark markings*

*Ankle joint, or hock, is high on the leg, which makes the leg very long and powerful*

### THE HARE AND THE DOG
The use of greyhounds for hare coursing – pursuing game with dogs that follow by sight, not scent – is probably one of the most ancient of all sports.

### BEAUTIFUL BOUNDER
The borzoi comes from Russia and used to be called the Russian wolfhound because it was used by the aristocracy for hunting and chasing wolves. The borzoi may have been developed from long-legged sight hounds (pp. 14–15), such as the Saluki, which were then crossed with long-haired, local, collie-type dogs. They were bred to look as aristocratic and beautiful as possible to match the noble aspirations of the Russian emperors.

# Hounds

Hounds are one of the most easily recognizable group of dogs, as they all have similar features – floppy ears, long muzzles, and powerful jaws. They are strong and hardy – even the more delicate-looking breeds – and are relentless hunters. Hounds hunt either by smell, like the bloodhound, or by sight, like the greyhound and Afghan hound. Sight hounds (pp. 14–15) have lightly built bodies, are fast runners, and are used in the hunt to chase prey. Scent hounds (pp. 16–17) are slower and more heavily built, and are used to sniff out prey; their long, droopy ears help guide the smells from the ground to the nose. Hounds vary in size more than any other dog group. The Irish wolfhound, a sight hound originally used for hunting wolves, is the heaviest of all dogs; the miniature dachshund, a scent hound used for hunting badgers, is one of the smallest. Many breeds of hound are still used today for hunting, but others, such as the wolfhound, are house dogs and companions. The lifespan of small hounds is around 15 years, but very large hounds live on average for only about half this time.

**ELEGANT BORZOI**
The borzoi (pp. 14–15) is the most aristocratic of all hounds, and it looks as though it would hardly deign to behave like an ordinary dog.

**WELSH LEGEND**
The town of Beddgelert in Wales is named after the famous deerhound Gelert, killed by Prince Llewellyn after he thought the dog had killed his child. The prince found blood all around the baby's cradle so he killed the dog with his sword. But then he found the baby safe, and nearby a dead wolf, killed by his faithful dog. This Welsh legend is one of several similar stories known in many countries around the world.

**LONG-HAIRED BEAUTY**
The Afghan hound is an ancient breed of long-haired greyhound that originated in Afghanistan, where it was used by the royal family for hunting gazelle (small antelope). After its arrival in Britain in the early 1900s, this dog was bred to be even longer-haired and more silky. The Afghan hound is a popular show dog but retains its hunting and racing instincts.

*Short hair on face and along the back*

*Very long, silky hair*

*Wrinkled brow and face*

*Long, silky ears*

*"Dewlap," or loose folds of skin hanging beneath its throat*

**TALLYHO**
The foxhound has changed little since medieval times; it is still used today for fox hunting. Foxhounds do not make good house dogs because for centuries they have been bred specifically for hunting and for living close together in large numbers as a pack.

**A DIGNIFIED DOG**
In modern times the role of the bloodhound has been that of a guard dog rather than a hunting hound, but its fearsome reputation as a relentless tracker has survived in legend if not in fact. Breeding for show standards has led to the folds of skin around its head becoming over-developed, and this can lead to health problems.

**THE HOUND OF THE BASKERVILLES**
Shown above is a still from one of three film versions of British writer Sir Arthur Conan Doyle's (1859–1930) famous Sherlock Holmes story.

*Tail is carried erect, not curled forward*

### THE GREAT DOG OF IRELAND
The ancient breed of hounds used in Ireland since medieval times for hunting wolves probably died out completely in the 19th century – more than 100 years after the last wolf was killed in Ireland. A British army officer recreated the breed in the late 1800s, and since then the Irish wolfhound has become a giant. It is the tallest dog in the world, with a shoulder height of up to 3 ft (94 cm). However, the old Irish wolfhound looked more like a rough-haired greyhound.

### HUNTING HARE
The beagle was originally bred for tracking hares in Britain and France, but it is now very popular in the U.S. and Canada, where it is used for hunting cottontail rabbits. Because they are small, have a uniform weight, and tolerate living together in large numbers, the beagle has become the breed most frequently used for laboratory research.

**A DEVONSHIRE HUNTING TAPESTRY**
This detail, from one of four Flemish tapestries woven in the early 1400s, shows a medieval hunting scene with richly dressed ladies and noblemen, their hounds, and prey of boar. These tapestries were once owned by the Duke of Devonshire in England.

### DON'T BADGER ME!
Dachshund means "badger dog" in German. This breed was originally an "earth dog" – a terrier used to dig out badgers from their dens. Because "hund" was translated into English as "hound," these dogs became classed in that group. The miniature dachshund is a popular house dog, weighing up to 12 lb (5.5 kg ).

*Straight, strong forelegs and long, muscular hindlegs enabled the Irish wolfhound to cover great distances in chasing its prey*

The dachshund can have three varieties of coat – short-haired, long-haired, or, as here, wire-haired

# Sporting dogs

*English setter holds a stick in its mouth, in the same way as it would a bird*

An object for training a sporting dog to become used to holding prey in its mouth

SPANIELS, SETTERS, pointers, and retrievers all fall within the category of dogs called "sporting dogs." Today, sporting dogs are mostly used to help hunters shoot game birds. For example, pointers and setters use their sharp eyes and keen noses to find the game. Then they point their body toward the bird and freeze, to guide the hunter. Sporting dogs must also have "soft" mouths so that they can fetch, or retrieve, the dead or wounded prey undamaged by their teeth (pp. 40–41). These breeds are not usually aggressive, having been originally bred to live together in kennels. They respond very well to training – for this reason they are raised not only for sport but also as house dogs and companions. The Labrador retriever is probably the most popular animal companion and helper dog (pp. 44–45) in the world.

**READY, AIM, FIRE**
Above all else, the hunter's dog must not be afraid of the noise of a gun.

*English setter's thick coat enables it to hunt in winter and to endure the cold weather*

**AT THE END OF THE DAY**
Along with their hunting dogs (pp. 40–41) and a horse, these hunters, wearing hacking jackets and riding breeches and holding their guns, are at rest after a long day's hunt.

**BRINGING HOME A BIRD**
The retriever is trained to retrieve (bring back to the hunter) game after it has been shot.

*Setters and pointers often hold up one front foot as they "freeze" into position before the shoot*

**RED-HAIRED BEAUTY**
The Irish, or red, setter has a silky coat and a gentle nature. However, the red setter is a high-strung and headstrong breed, and it is often considered to be unreliable as a sporting dog.

## A REAL CHARMER

Although it is now a show dog and pet, the cocker spaniel was bred as a sporting dog and got its name from its ability to flush out birds called woodcocks.

*Muscular, strong-boned legs helped the cocker to be an excellent bird dog*

## A DAMP DAY FOR DUCK HUNTING

Duck shooting often ends up with both the hunter and his dog getting very wet. Spaniels, which have been bred for hundreds of years as water dogs, are the traditional companions of the duck hunter. This painting (above) shows a Chesapeake retriever, a curly-coated retriever, and an Irish water spaniel (from left to right).

## GETTING THE POINT

Pointers are trained to "point" (pp. 16–17) at hidden game with their noses. This makes them essential companions on bird shoots.

Dog made of Italian glass decorates lid of Austrian box, c.1800

*Tail is called "feathered" when it looks like the feathers of a bird*

## GOOD SHOT

This 18th-century tile from France shows a hunter – wearing a shoulder pouch for collecting the game – and his dogs chasing the prey, which is probably a rabbit or a hare.

## SETTING UP THE GAME

The English setter is one of the oldest breeds of sporting dogs. Originally, the setter was a spaniel that was trained to "set" the game – to go into bushes to scare, or spring, birds into the air so that they could be killed. In the Middle Ages birds were caught in nets; later they were shot with guns. This setter is holding a stick in its mouth in the same way that it would hold a dead bird.

Special long lead allows sporting dogs to escape their leash quickly

# Terriers

**TARTAN TERRIER**
The modern Scottish terrier, or "Scottie," is descended from short-legged, rough-coated working terriers that were bred for centuries in the Scottish Highlands. The Scottie was not typically black until the 1900s.

T ERRIERS ARE KNOWN AS "EARTH DOGS"– *terra* means "the earth" in Latin. They are great diggers and need no encouragement to go down holes in the ground in pursuit of burrowing animals such as foxes, rabbits, and rats. Terriers have an ancient history in Britain and have always been used as sporting and hunting dogs. They are the best dogs for killing rats on farms and in mines. Traditionally, many types of terriers have been bred in various regions of Britain – like the Border, Scottish, and Yorkshire terriers – but a few other countries have also developed new breeds, such as the Australian terrier. Many of the terriers registered by the kennel clubs of today have been distinguished as separate breeds only in the last hundred years.

*The tip of the Airedale's small, V-shaped ear falls forward to the top of its eye*

*Strong teeth and vicelike jaws prevent prey from escaping*

*Coat is stiff and wiry and lies close to the body; it requires careful grooming (pp. 62–63)*

*Long, strong jaws help the Australian terrier catch rabbits, rats, and even snakes*

**A SHAGGY DOG STORY**
Early British immigrants to Australia took their dogs with them, and by the early 1900s this new breed – the Australian terrier – had been developed from a mix of cairn, Dandie Dinmont, Irish, Scottish, and Yorkshire terriers.

**A ROMAN DOG**
Discovered in northern England during the 1800s, this copper alloy figure (made between the first and fourth centuries A.D.) looks like an old terrier breed – the Aberdeen.

*The ears of the low-slung, compact Norfolk terrier are slightly rounded at the tip and drop forward close to its cheek*

*Given a rubber ring or ball, the playful nature of a terrier is quite apparent*

## A GIANT AMONG TERRIERS

The Airedale terrier is named after the district in Yorkshire, England, where it originated. The largest of all terriers, it was developed in the mid-1800s by crossbreeding (pp. 60–61) the now-extinct black and tan terrier with the otterhound to increase its size and strength for the hunting of large prey. The Airedale was also used in World War I as a messenger dog (pp. 44–45).

*Tail is set high and carried erect, not curved forward over its back*

### A LEGEND IN HIS OWN LIFETIME

When a gentleman named Greyfriars died in Edinburgh, Scotland, his faithful little dog – a Skye-type terrier called Bobby – refused to leave his master's grave until he himself died, ten years later. So the legend of "Greyfriars' Bobby" began.

### DECORATED "DRUMMER" DOG

Dogs have always been popular as mascots. Shown here is the brave war hero, Drummer, the mascot of an English army regiment, the Northumberland Fusiliers. Drummer's death was reported in a British newspaper in 1902.

### DIGGER BONES

The Norfolk terrier is a new breed that is descended from terriers bred in East Anglia, England. It is an active little dog with short legs and a wiry coat. This terrier used to be called a Norwich terrier, which had both prick, and drop-eared varieties, but in 1965 the name of Norfolk was given to those with drop ears.

### FOXY FELLOW

In the late 1800s, the fox terrier was the most popular breed of dog in England. Today this popularity has been taken over by the smaller Jack Russell terrier (pp. 38–39). Fox terriers can be either wire-haired like this one, or smooth-haired.

*With excellent balance, a wire-haired fox terrier is ready for action – whether tearing up a carpet or hunting foxes (pp. 28–29)*

*Bedlington's long ears, pear-shaped head, and curly, light-colored coat make it look more like a lamb*

### LIKE A LAMB

All sorts of breeds, including the whippet, otterhound, and bull terrier are thought to have contributed to the development of the Bedlington terrier, at one time known as the Rothbury terrier.

### DANDIFIED DOG

Dogs have been used in advertising for a long time. Here, a terrier in his finery graces a magazine cover.

*Terriers – like this Norfolk – dig with both their front and hind legs*

# Nonsporting dogs

**MADE IN AMERICA**
The Boston terrier is a very popular dog and is one of the few breeds to have been developed in the U.S.

NONSPORTING DOGS is a miscellaneous collection of dogs that includes the ones left over after all the other breeds have been neatly categorized into the other five groups (pp. 48–53, 56–59). The title of "special dogs" might be more apt to describe the range of individual, and special, characteristics, as this group includes some of the more unusual dogs. The history of some nonsporting dogs goes back for many centuries – the forerunner of the chow chow was first bred 3,000 years ago in Mongolia, Asia, for use in war, and later, in China, as a source of fur and food. In fact, most of the dogs in this group were originally bred for work or sport but are now kept primarily as pets and show dogs. For example, at one time French hunters sent poodles to retrieve ducks; bulldogs were once bred for baiting bulls (pp. 46–47); and Dalmatians were used for herding cattle and hunting game. This group also includes national dogs from various countries – the Boston terrier from the United States, the bulldog from Britain, and the poodle from France.

**USEFUL HELPERS**
In this detail from a 17th-century Japanese screen, a richly dressed Portuguese merchant is shown with his servants and faithful companion – his dog.

*The back has retained the powerful muscles of the old-fashioned bulldog*

**BAT-EARED BULLDOG**
In the old days French bulldogs were used for baiting donkeys (pp. 46–47). Today they are smaller and live more peaceful lives, but it is still a tough breed and a good guard dog.

*Legs are set wide apart, allowing the dog to stand its ground*

French bulldog

**CHINESE CHOW**
The breed of chow chow is now 200 years old, having been developed from a pair of dogs of pariah origin (pp. 36–37) introduced into England from Canton in southeast China in the 1780s. English naturalist Gilbert White (1720–1793) in his *Natural History and Antiquities of Selborne* (1789) described the dogs as "such as are fattened in that country for the purpose of being eaten."

*Very thick fur and curled tails are typical of spitz dogs, like the chow chow, for adapting to sub-Arctic temperatures*

*The tongue of the chow chow is always blue-black, an unusual characteristic inherited from the dog's Chinese ancestors*

**THE BEST OF BRITISH**
The bulldog is the national symbol of the British, portraying strength and stubbornness. This breed was developed for baiting bulls – setting dogs on bulls for public sport – and dates back to at least the 16th century.

### JUMPING THROUGH HOOPS

Because the poodle is one of the most easily trained of breeds, it has been commonly used as a circus dog. In this fine gold brooch, made in Austria c.1890, a clown encourages his troop of dogs to perform tricks.

*Muzzle is adorned by a massive mustache*

This strongest of all the schnauzers – the giant schnauzer – stands up to 2 ft (65 cm) at the shoulder

### BUSHY-HAIRED BEAUTY

Schnauzers got their name from the German word *Schnauze*, meaning "muzzle." Originally used for herding sheep in southern Germany, nowadays these energetic dogs make excellent companions and family pets. In the U.S. and Canada the giant and standard schnauzers are classified as working dogs (pp. 56–57), and the miniature is in the terrier group (pp. 52–53).

### THE ELEGANT "COACH DOG"

In the 1800s, it was very fashionable in England and France to have a "coach dog" to accompany the carriages of aristocrats. The horses' harness and dog's coat colors were coordinated.

*The Dalmatian's coat is always pure white with distinctive black or brown (liver) spots*

### SPOTTED DOG

There are several legends about the origin of Dalmatians. Some people believe that these dogs came from India with gypsies who settled in Dalmatia, now Yugoslavia; others think that the breed originated in Italy. Dalmatians were first brought to England by travelers to Europe in the 18th century. It then became fashionable to have these aristocratic-looking dogs running beside the carriage horses of gentlemen. The Dalmatian is unique in that it excretes urea, and not uric acid, in its urine. This means that it should be a popular breed with gardeners because its urine does not kill lawn grass.

*Legs are long and built for speed and endurance*

### PRETTY AS A PICTURE

Poodles were first bred as sporting dogs (pp. 50–51), probably in Germany, but their intelligence and attractive appearance soon led to their chief role of much-loved house dog. An early form of the pet poodle as it was in the 1700s is shown in this painting by Jean Jacques Bachelier (1724–1806).

# Working dogs

**SUPERIOR SWIMMER**
The huge Newfoundland breed may originate from Pyrenean mountain rescue dogs taken to Newfoundland in eastern Canada by Spanish fishermen.

**ROYAL CORGI**
Since medieval times in Wales there have been short-legged cattle dogs, called corgis, that are now favorites of British royalty.

T HE EARLIEST DOMESTIC DOGS (pp. 34–35) were companions to human hunters in their pursuit of all sorts of animals from mammoths to small birds. Over the thousands of years since that time, dogs have always worked with people. Before Europeans reached North America in the 15th century A.D., the dog was the only animal that had been domesticated by American Indians. The primary work of these dogs was to draw a travois, or sled, laden with possessions when a family moved from place to place. They were also used to help in the great bison hunts when a whole herd of bison could be driven to its death. Eskimo dogs and huskies have been indispensable in polar exploration. In Europe, where there have been horses and oxen for pulling carts, dogs have not been as commonly used for this type of work. For the purposes of dog shows, the breed registry includes herding dogs (pp. 42–43) and helper dogs (pp. 44–45) in the category of working dogs.

**AGILE AUSSIE**
The job of the Australian kelpie is to round up sheep that have strayed from the main flock – it has the odd ability of running along sheep's backs to reach the head of the flock. A well-trained dog can do the work of six men, and it is able to travel 40 miles (64 km) in a day.

*Color of a husky's eyes can be brown or blue – or even one of each*

Siberian husky

*Dogs lose heat through their tongues, which is why they pant to cool down – even in the Arctic*

*Thick ruff of fur around neck and stocky shape keep as much warmth as possible inside the husky's body*

**SWISS BLANKET**
The Bernese mountain dog, a typical helper dog (pp. 44–45), is an example of many breeds of mastiff-type dogs that have been used throughout Europe and Asia since the Roman period for guarding and protecting travelers in the mountains. By sleeping beside the traveler at night, the dog's exceptionally thick fur would keep both human and animal warm, and by day the dog would be able to follow the path with its nose, even through thick snow.

**SPECIAL DELIVERY**
In Switzerland and other very mountainous countries, mastiff-type dogs were the best animals for drawing milk carts steadily along narrow paths. From the earliest times (pp. 34–35), the mastiff's natural aggression made it an excellent guard dog.

The word "Eskimo" means "snow." It is no longer used for the Inuit and other native North Americans who live in the Arctic regions, but the name has remained in use for their dogs.

*The Great Dane, like all mastiffs, has a very deep and powerful chest*

*The working dog's harness is designed to give it the greatest pulling power*

**WHEN IS A DANE NOT A DANE?**
The Great Dane was developed in Germany, where in the old days no castle was complete without a pair of these giant mastiff-type dogs to guard it.

*The tail trails when the dog is working or at rest, but curves over its back when the dog is running*

**HARNESSING A HUSKY**
The Siberian husky is the only pure breed of this dog. Otherwise, the name is used in North America, particularly Canada, for all the dogs of the spitz type that are used for drawing sleds and for hunting seals and other Arctic animals. Peoples who have lived for thousands of years in the Arctic zones of North America, Europe, and Asia could not have survived without their working huskies and Eskimo dogs (pp. 46–47).

**HERALDIC DOG**
Images of dogs have often appeared in heraldry. This husky is an important part of the coat of arms for Canada's Yukon Territory.

# Toy dogs

Dismal Desmond
– a popular stuffed toy
from the 1930s in England
– lives up to his name

THE CATEGORY OF TOY DOGS INCLUDES all the smallest show breeds. Most dogs in this group have a height of less than 12 in (30.5 cm). Perhaps one of the most remarkable facts of all about the domestication of animals is that even every toy dog, however small, is descended from the wolf. Because, genetically, it has inherited the same characteristics as its wild ancestor, even the tiniest dog will try its best to behave like a wolf. It will gnaw at bones, guard its territory, and show its feelings to other dogs with its posture and tail – just as a wolf does. The Romans were probably the first to breed miniature dogs, and bones of dogs that are as small as any of today's breeds have been found on Roman excavations. The small white dogs known as Maltese (pp. 10–11) are probably of Roman origin, and dogs of this type often appear in Roman paintings. Other tiny dogs have been bred since ancient times in Tibet, China, and Japan. In Europe, toy spaniels were the favorite companions of the aristocracy throughout the Middle Ages.

*Small, V-shaped ears set high on head*

*Fine, silky-textured coat is long except on face and ears*

**DOG'S DINNER**
In a detail from this charming, 19th-century French painting, entitled *Caninemania*, the family pet is treated as a very special dinner guest – to the exclusion of the lady's friend who has been relegated to a seat in the corner – and is, therefore, out of the picture.

*Large, broad head with flat profile and snub nose*

**TOY TERRIER TERROR**
The Australian silky terrier is not a toy by nature. This short-legged, compact dog can kill a rat or a rabbit in seconds, and it is claimed to be equally quick at killing snakes. Although it looks a little like a Yorkshire terrier, this breed is reputed to have originated entirely by crossbreeding in Australia.

**CHINESE LION DOG**
Another name for the Pekingese is the "lion dog of Peking." There is a legend that these dogs were first bred to represent the lion spirit of Buddha. Today the Pekingese, with its big eyes, round head, flat face, and soft fur looks more like a cuddly toy than a lion.

A Pekingese walks with a side-to-side rolling gait, trying to distribute its weight evenly on its short legs

**PEKINGESE PAIR**
Miniature dogs have existed in China for at least 2,500 years, but the Pekingese itself is probably not a very ancient breed. The Pekingese was kept as a palace dog by the Imperial family of Peking (now Beijing). It was introduced to the West by English forces who looted the Imperial Palace in 1860; since that time the breed has become smaller and more short-legged.

## A POPULAR PINSCHER

The miniature pinscher is a much older breed than its larger cousin, the Doberman pinscher. As with the Doberman, show standards specify that the tail of the breed must be docked (pp. 44–45), a practice that prevents the dog from expressing its emotions naturally and upsets its balance when running.

*Head is well rounded with a turned-up nose*

## ROYAL FAVORITE

Probably originating in China or Japan, this good-tempered little dog arrived in England from France in the 16th century. It was Charles II's great fondness for this dog that gave the breed its name.

*The miniature pinscher is no softy and has the strong legs of a much larger dog*

King Charles spaniel

## PAINTED POMERANIAN

In the 18th century, when English artist Thomas Gainsborough (1727–1788) painted this Pomeranian mother with her puppy, the breed was much larger than it is today. The Pomeranian is a miniature spitz and has the stocky body, pricked ears, ruff of fur, and curled tail that is typical of this group of northern dogs (pp. 46–47).

*The tail of the Bichon is always curled over its back*

## BICHON FRISE

Within recent years the Bichon Frise (meaning "curly lap-dog") has become increasingly popular, especially in the U.S. The Bichon is a Franco-Belgian breed, much like a small poodle, and though it looks, literally, like a toy, it is a lively, playful little dog.

*The white coat has a very soft woolly underfur and an upper layer of loosely curled silky hairs*

# Crossbred dogs

THE DEVELOPMENT OF BREEDS OF DOG for different purposes, such as hunting (pp. 40–41), herding (pp. 42–43), guarding (pp. 44–45), and sport (pp. 46–47), has been a long, slow process that has continued over more than 5,000 years. However, most of the dogs in the world are still mongrels, or crossbred dogs. These are dogs that have interbred with each other at random, as opposed to purebred dogs (pp. 48–59), which are dogs of the same breed that have been selectively bred by humans. It is possible for all 400 breeds of dogs in the world to interbreed, because they are all descended from the wolf (pp. 8–9) and, therefore, they all belong to one species. It would obviously be difficult, from a practical point of view, for a Great Dane to mate with a tiny Pekingese. However, many unlikely crosses have occurred – such as a dachshund with a German shepherd. It is often claimed that crossbred dogs are more intelligent than purebred dogs, but it is more likely that their behavior just shows more variation because they combine good characteristics of a number of different breeds.

**SITTING DOG**
This mongrel is eagerly waiting for its reward.

*Tail arched upward helps dog retain its balance*

**ONE GIANT LEAP FOR DOGKIND**
These five pictures (right) show the actions used by this crossbred dog in jumping over an obstacle. The tail is particularly important for keeping the dog's balance.

*Strong, well-muscled legs help this dog jump high off the ground at the beginning of its leap*

Correct stance for getting ready to take off

**GOOD DOG!**
Training a dog to establish good behavior patterns can be a long and arduous process, as this child realizes – but both will get their rewards in the end.

**"HIS MASTER'S VOICE"**
This painting by English artist Francis Barraud (1856–1924) was bought by the British gramophone company EMI for $180. The dog, "Nipper," was the artist's own, and he was a crossbreed with a lot of bull terrier in him. This charming picture and its slogan were first registered as a trademark in 1910, and are still known in the U.S. as a sign of RCA records.

*Strong, well-proportioned legs*

**ON THE DOGHOUSE**
Snoopy – the world's favorite cartoon dog – is mainly a beagle with a bit of something else too. Many amusing adventures befall him each week in comic strips, but – like most dogs – he likes to sleep and dream, especially on top of his doghouse.

## WAITING FOR A FRIEND

A dog's wagging tail is seen as a friendly gesture toward either humans or other animals. This small figure of a pet dog, made of terra cotta in 500 B.C., was found in Boeotia, in central Greece.

## DOGS' BEST FRIEND

This poignant painting, entitled *L'Ami des Bêtes*, by French artist Constantin Magnier, was published in 1910. It shows an old tramp sharing his small amount of food with his only friends – a large group of mongrels.

*Alert ears*

*Eyes looking straight ahead*

*Mouth open for more air*

## KEEPING ITS COOL

This crossbred puppy (pp. 20–21) is licking its nose to help keep cool on a hot summer's day.

*Bright, alert eyes*

*Medium-length coat – neither too short, nor too long*

*Tail arches over back when dog touches down*

*Well-defined body outline*

*Front legs are straight and feet firmly on the ground when jump is completed*

*Well-shaped nose*

*Pert, expressive ears*

## A MOTLEY CREW

These crossbred dogs are without any extremes of physical form or function, and they will provide companionship, friendship, and loyalty for their owners. Aside from their individual endearing qualities, crossbreeds are often tougher, better-tempered, less disease-prone, and more adaptable than their pedigree counterparts.

# Caring for a dog

1. Ready and waiting for a grooming session

OWNERSHIP OF A DOG should be taken on only by people who are prepared to keep the animal for the whole of its life – up to 17 years. For the first year, training a puppy is not very different from bringing up a child, and in some ways it is much easier, as a dog can be housebroken much faster than a child can be potty-trained. The dog's every need must be attended to, but at the same time it must be taught to take its place within its human family. A dog should never be left on its own for more than a few hours. It requires clean drinking water, regular meals at set times, and hard biscuits or bones to chew on, to keep its teeth clean. Every dog should be treated for internal and external parasites, such as tapeworms and fleas, and inoculated against diseases such as distemper and, in countries where it occurs, rabies.

**BATHTIME FOR BONZO**
This little girl is intent on keeping her pet clean.

2. A partially clipped poodle

3. Fine-tuning underneath

**TICKLISH TAPERING**
Originally the poodle was a water dog (pp. 54–55), and its coat was clipped to keep it from getting matted. Today, most poodles are companion animals, but even so the coat should be clipped for the dog's comfort rather than for show standards.

4. Very wet poodle after its bath

5. Perfecting the tail

6. The end result

Bowl of water at all times

Dish of dry, crunchy dog food

Assortment of dog biscuits

Essential aids for looking after a dog

*Dense coat of a poodle needs extra-special grooming*

Brush and comb

Favorite toys

Rawhide bone

Lead

Collar

### AND SO TO BED
In the same way that a wild wolf will have its own den, every domestic dog needs a bed of its own. This can be a basket, or a beanbag, or an old armchair that the dog has taken over for itself.

Cleaning the teeth

Clipping the claws

Trimming hair between the claws

### THE WINNER IS
Dog shows have been held for the last hundred years. The exhibition of dogs at shows keeps up the standards of the breeds and allows all the people concerned to meet and discuss their achievements and problems. However, the points of the breeds as set for showing are not always in the dog's best interests – for example docking the tail (pp. 44–45) removes a most important means of communication for the dog, as well as upsetting its balance when it runs.

### STRAY DOGS
The most frightening event that can happen to a dog is to be lost or abandoned by its owner. If the lost dog is taken to a home for stray dogs, it will become extremely anxious and confused. A dog should never be turned out onto the street. If it can no longer be kept, nor a new home found for it, as a last resort the kindest thing to do is to have it put to sleep by a veterinary surgeon.

NAME.......... TEL.......
ADDRESS.................

### IDENTIFICATION
Every dog must carry its owner's name and address. This can be engraved on a tag attached to the dog's collar, or it can be as a code in a small tattoo, or by a tiny coded pellet under the skin.

# Index

# Acknowledgments

**Dorling Kindersley would like to thank:**
Trevor Smith's Animal World, V. Battarby, R. Hills, E. Mustoe, H. Neave, D. Peach, R. Ramphul, S. Renton, S. Surrell, J. Williamson, and J. Young for lending dogs for photography.
The zoos of Augsburg, Duisburg, and Osnabrück for providing wild dogs for photography.
J. Larner for grooming section.
The British Kennel Club and Mrs. R. Wilford for breed information.
The Natural History Museum's staff and R. Loverance of the British Museum for their research help.
J. Gulliver for her help in the initial stages of the book.
C. Carez, B. Crowley, C. Gillard, T. Keenes, and E. Sephton for their editorial/design assistance.
J. Parker for the index.

**Illustrations:**
E. Sephton, J. Kaiser-Atcherley

**Picture credits**
t=top b=bottom c=center l=left r=right

Advertising Archives: 60bl, 63bl
Allsport: 46cl; /Bob Martin: 15cr
American Museum of Natural/ A. E. Anderson: 9tl; /Logan: 9ct
Ancient Art and Architecture Collection: 49bcl
Animal Photography/Sally Anne Thompson: 39tr, 45tr, 45br, 50c
Ardea, London/Eric Dragesco: 25tl; /Ian Beames: 35br; /Jean-Paul Ferrero: 22t, 37cl, 56c; /Kenneth W. Fink: 20bl, 31br; /M. Krishnan: 36cbl; /S. Meyers: 28tl
Australian Overseas Information Service, London: 37tr
Bridgeman Art Library: 6tl, 6–7t, 7tr, 40cl, 41tl, 41tr, 42tr; Cadogan Gallery, London: 18cl; Oldham Art Gallery, Lancs: 46tr; Rafael Valls Gallery, London: 55bl
British Museum: 34tl, 34br, 35cl, 35bl; Museum of Mankind: 26br
Jean-Loup Charmet: 19bl, 51bl, 58cr, 61tr
Bruce Coleman/John M. Burnley: 19tl; /Jessica Ehlers: 36bl; /Jeff Foott: 32cl; /Gullivan & Rogers: 33br; /F. Jorge: 32tr; /Leonard Lee Rue: 25tc, 29tl
Columbia Pictures Television: 39tl
Sylvia Cordaiy Photo Library: 63cr
Cyanamid (UK)/Animal Health Div.: 11b
C. M. Dixon: 36tl
EMI Records: 60cr
English Heritage/Keith Hobbs: 52cr
e.t. Archive: 48bl
Mary Evans Picture Library: back jacket cl, 10tl, 16bl, 21c, 22cb, 44bl, 47bl, 48tl, 48tr, 53tc
Marc Henrie, ASC (London): 42br
© Hergé: 47cr
Michael Holford: front jacket br, 4br, 34bl, 38cl, 58bl
Hutchison Library/H. R. Dörig: 32tl; /R. Ian Lloyd: 35tl
ILN Picture Library: 53cl, 56br
Image Bank: 12tl, 30tl
Imperial War Museum: 44tr
Dave King: 10br, 13ctl, 39 btr, 42 bl, 45cr, 48cl, 51tl, 52tl, 52–53tl, 53c, 54tr, 54bl, 57tl, 61bl
Kobal Collection: 42tl; /Avco Embassy: 23br; /Twentieth Century Fox: 49tl
Michael Leach: 29cb
Leeds Castle Enterprises Ltd.: 35bc
Macmillan Inc.: 8br
National Archive of Canada/ Karen E. Bailey (C–137830): 57b
National Portrait Gallery: 56tr
Natural History Museum Pubs.: 9br
Peter Newark's Pictures: 25c, 29cr
NHPA/Michael Leach: 36ctl; /Mandal Raijit: 27bl
Robert Opie Collection: 44tl, 50tl, 54cr, 62tl
Oxford Scientific Films/O. Newman: 25cr
Planet Earth Pictures/J. R. Bracegirdle: 24bc; /Jim Brandenburg: 11cr, 23bl; /J. Scott: 21tl
Axel Poignant Archive: 36br
Retrograph Archive/Martin Breese: 14tr, 20tl, 42cl, 44br, 46tl, 50cl, 53cr
Gary Santry: 61cr
Science Photo Library/John Sanford: 8tl
South American Pictures/Tony Morrison: 33bl
Tate Gallery: 59tr
Tring Museum: 7bl
© 1990 United Feature Syndicate, Inc.: 60br
F. R. Valla: 35cr
V & A Museum: 29br, 56tl, 58tl
Werner Forman Archive: 23ct, 24tr, 41tc, 54tl
Zefa Picture Library: 47cl
© Dr. Erik Zimen: 18ctr, 19tr, 21cl, 23tr